BADLAND BRIDE
Dakota Hearts, Book Two
Lisa Mondello

Badland Bride

Dakota Hearts, Volume 2

Lisa Mondello

Published by Lisa Mondello, 2015.

Badland Bride

Copyright © 2013 Lisa Mondello

License:

This eBook is licensed for your personal enjoyment only. The work is protected by copyright law from theft and unauthorized distribution. No part of this book can be used, copied, or published in whole or in part in any form without the expressed written permission of the author. This eBook may not be re-sold or given away to other people unless it is part of the lending program. If you're reading this book and did not purchase it, or it was not purchased for lending through an authorized vendor, then please delete it from your device and purchase your own copy. Thank you for respecting the author's work by not participating in unauthorized distribution.

BADLAND BRIDE

First edition. October 23, 2015.

ISBN: 979-8227548450

Written by Lisa Mondello.

Description

RAISED AN ARMY BRAT, Regis Simpson was used to calling new towns home, learning to quickly make friends but never letting anyone get too close. When devastating floods tear through the Badlands of South Dakota, she thinks Rudolph is just another town that needs to be rebuilt. Nothing more. The sooner she gets her work done, the sooner the people of Rudolph can heal and she can move on to the next town in need. She never counted on the sexy town doctor, Keith "Hawk" McKinnon or his determination to break down walls she'd spent a lifetime building, making it impossible for her to leave.

Nothing pained Hawk McKinnon more than seeing people he'd known his whole life hurting. He traded a high-paying salary at a city hospital to come back to Rudolph and make a difference where he'd dug his roots. When the beautiful Regis Simpson comes to town offering help, he's immediately drawn to her even though she's spent a lifetime packing armor around her heart. But once her work is done, she'll be leaving again. He's determined to do everything possible to make her stay.

Chapter One

ARMY BRATS WEREN'T wusses. She'd been dealing with tough situations from the moment she'd pushed her way into the world. At least that's what Regis Simpson's daddy always told her. She should've known better than to traipse through mud and rubble without proper boots, no matter how stylish her flats looked in the store window. Her reward was the nice chunk of metal from the rusty fence that had somehow embedded itself into her ankle when she'd slipped.

"You're going to need a tetanus shot for that."

Regis looked up at the man standing over her. He'd just taken her on a thirty minute walk around his property to assess flood damage. It wasn't pretty. Now, as she was sprawled out on the muddy ground, smelling earth and Lord knows what else decaying, she tried to focus on the wetness from the ground seeping into the fabric of her pants rather than the pain in her leg.

"I'm up on my shots," she said, trying her best not to pass out as she pulled her leg away from the twisted fence.

Regis took the man's proffered hands in hers and welcomed his help. She'd already been out to six properties today and couldn't remember all the people she'd talked to.

Tim Bennett. That was this guy's name, right? Relief flooded her. She hated when her brain became overloaded with details. And Mr. Bennett had bigger worries than the damage she'd done to her leg to help keep her straight. Everyone in Rudolph and the surrounding towns in the Badlands of South Dakota were worried about whether or not insurance would cover enough to repair the damage to their property after the worst ice storms and flooding in a hundred years had swept through the area. That's what she did, and the only reason she was on a marathon tour of destruction. And there were days she wondered why she was still doing it after five straight years of living out of a suitcase and calling the local motel in Anytown, USA her home.

"No, you really should have Hawk take a look at that. It looks pretty bad. Might need stitches."

"Hawk? What is he, a local Native American shaman or something?"

Mr. Bennett smiled. "More like the local daredevil. Or he used to be anyway. People around here joke he went into medicine just so he could stitch up his own wounds because the thieving insurance companies cancelled his policy."

The joke fell flat, and Mr. Bennett's smile immediately faltered as if he suddenly remembered who he was speaking to. "Let me see if I can find something clean to wrap that leg."

"I'd appreciate that."

Regis couldn't exactly blame Mr. Bennett for being nervous. It didn't matter what town she was in across America. When a natural disaster struck an area, it caused upheaval and destruction that she needed to help these fine folks fix. She was their hope of a swift recovery ... so long as she approved their claim.

And that, she was sure, was the reason for Mr. Bennett's nervous energy.

While she waited, she carefully tried to put weight on her foot but felt warm moisture seep into her shoe as pain shot up her leg. She quietly let out a colorful stream of expletives that she knew sounded odd coming out of the mouth of someone in her position. But being raised by a single father on Army bases around the world, she heard a thing or two that made even her toes curl.

Mr. Bennett handed Regis a couple of paper towels. "I found these in the car. They're clean."

"Thank you," Regis tried not to wince as she placed the paper towel on her leg. It was no use. She stood and carefully tried to put weight on her foot again. Her ankle throbbed, but she forced herself to walk on it so she could get to her car. Once there, she leaned up against the car door and hiked up her pant leg to get a better look at her injury.

"You're definitely going to need stitches for that," Mr. Bennett said.

Feeling queasy, she asked, "You wouldn't happen to have that Hawk doctor's address on you, would you?"

"No need for an address. Just stay on this road until you get to the center of town. Turn left at the diner and it's right across the street. You can't miss it. It's the only clinic in town."

"Turn left at the diner. That sounds easy enough. Does this Hawk have a real name?"

Mr. Bennett smiled. "His sign says Dr. Keith McKinnon. But I don't know anyone who calls him that."

"Hawk? Right, thanks," Regis muttered to herself as she eased her body into the driver's seat. Once inside, she closed her eyes to the dizziness she felt. She had to drive to town, find this doctor's office and hope this Hawk doctor could take care of her wound quickly. With her long lists of properties to assess, she couldn't afford down time.

As her engine fired up, Mr. Bennett said, "Ah, what about my claim?"

"I'll get back to you on that. I have the information for your paperwork." Despite the cold March wind outside, beads of sweat bubbled up on her forehead.

He looked worried. "Phone service is knocked out."

"I'll be setting up an office at the senior center by the end of the week. You can check in with me there."

That is, she'd have an office if the senior center allowed her the space. She hadn't heard back on that yet. Otherwise, she'd be seeing clients in the motel parking lot.

As she drove towards the center of town, Regis tried not to look at the devastation around her. There were days she felt numb to it, having seen so much in the five years she'd worked at her job. But she couldn't help but feel for the people who were suffering here. She passed a farm that had all its fields washed out. There were ruts in the mud, most likely caused by a tractor that had picked up debris and animals that hadn't made it in the flood. A barn that had once seen its glory days of use was now caved in on one side due to erosion of the foundation from water damage.

She tried not to look as she drove because she knew what everyone else here didn't know. Not everyone would get what they needed. Not everyone would recover from this. And those who'd get bad news, would get it from her.

A series of ice storms, and then an unseasonably high amount of rain, had caused massive flooding throughout South Dakota. The area around the Black Hills had been hit particularly hard. Her office had been inundated with insurance claims from thousands of people reporting property damage. She, as well as a dozen of her colleagues, had been on the road for weeks, examining the damage and submitting paperwork to approve each claim so people could rebuild.

She saw the diner she'd eaten breakfast at that morning and hit her blinker for a left turn. The clinic was easy to miss being nothing more than an old farmhouse that had a fresh coat of paint and a handicap ramp newly installed out front. If not for the felled tree that had been recently cut into pieces and stacked neatly next to the parking lot, if you could call it that, she would have missed the sign.

She parked her car in the empty parking lot. "Maybe this will be quick, and I can get back on the road."

After easing herself out of the car, she limped up the newly built wooden ramp, unpainted and still sporting the color of wood that hadn't been exposed to the elements for long. She winced through the pain as she took each step toward the front door. A small sign hung next to the door giving the clinic's hours. She tried the door, and it wouldn't budge. Her shoulders sagged in defeat.

"What does he do in the middle of the day? Go fishing?"

"Nope, house calls."

Regis swung around to see a tall man walking up behind her on the ramp. He had the Irish blue eyes she'd seen on many models in advertising magazines she'd bought when she was a teenager, and the dark hair that looked a little unruly in the wind, but seemed to fit him perfectly. The light scuff of a beard wasn't more than a day old, but already dark and covering his square jaw.

For a moment, Regis was so taken with this handsome stranger that she'd forgotten why she was there.

"DR. HAWK, OR WHATEVER his name actually is, does house calls? I thought that sort of thing went extinct with the dinosaurs. The guy must be a hundred years old."

Hawk fought to keep from smiling. "There are days it seems that way." He then looked at the woman's leg and frowned as he saw the blood staining her pants. "We'd better get you inside so that can be cleaned."

"The door's locked," the woman said, leaning against the rail as he came up beside her. Her face was pale, most probably due to the pain she was experiencing and the loss of blood.

He smiled, looking down into her eyes. "Luckily, I have a key." They were pretty brown eyes, he decided. No, they were hazel. And the fact that he didn't want her to turn away so he could know for sure surprised him.

Standing six feet tall, he towered over her small frame, although he was probably no more than eight inches taller than her. And she smelled like fresh soap as if she'd just taken a shower. But looking at the dirt and blood on her hands, that probably wasn't the case.

"You must rate to have your own key to the doctor's office. When does this Hawk doctor usually come back?"

He slipped the key into the door and turned the handle. Then he smiled as he pushed the door open and held it for her to come inside. "Why don't you have a seat here. It'll just be a minute."

Hawk curled his fingers around the woman's upper arm gently and helped guide her to the chair. As she sat down, a look of relief washed over her face.

"Does that take some pressure off?"

"What?"

"Your leg. Does sitting help?"

As he waited for her to reply, he walked behind the receptionist desk and sifted through the wall organizer that was filled with insurance forms. Nancy was going to have a fit if he had this woman fill out the wrong one.

"Ah, a little."

He felt a muscle pull between his eyebrows as he glanced at the forms. For all his higher education, insurance forms were a mystery to him. Finally, he sighed and dropped the papers on the desk.

"I'm going to need you to fill out some forms, but I'm not sure which one's right at the moment, and my receptionist, Nancy, will have my hide if I have you fill out the wrong form. So why don't we just have a look at your leg first and fill out paperwork later?"

"Your receptionist?"

"Yes. She'll probably be back from lunch before I'm done."

"You? Wait, you're Dr. Hawk?"

His lips curled up just slightly. "It's just Hawk. But if you prefer, you can call me Dr. McKinnon."

Her mouth hung open just slightly. "Oh, I'm ... oh, okay."

"Did someone tell you I was a deranged killer?"

"What? No, of course not, it's just ..."

She was adorable, all flustered with her flub. Hawk couldn't resist teasing her. "They said I was a mean old bastard who was going to cut off your leg?"

She rolled her eyes. "Don't be ridiculous."

"Then what?"

"You aren't ... I wasn't expecting someone so ..." She took a deep breath.

"So ... handsome?"

Color immediately stained her pale cheeks. "Young. You look like you just graduated college."

He chuckled. "So they didn't tell you I was good looking. They told you I was old."

She sighed heavily. "No. Mr. Bennett didn't say anything except your name is Hawk. What kind of person walks around with a name like that anyway?"

"Me," he said. "And I can assure you that you are in good hands. I may not be a crusty old doctor, but I not only went to college, I made it all the way through med school, my internship and a stint at the city hospital in Sioux Falls before coming back to Rudolph and starting my practice here."

Her shoulders slumped. "I didn't mean to imply—"

"Let's get you cleaned up," he said. "Let me help you—"

He bent down to help her to her feet, and he caught a whiff of her soapy scent again. Normally he didn't notice such things. But he was having a hard time not noticing every little detail about this woman from the slight hook of her nose to the patch of too many freckles on her left cheek.

"No, I can do it."

"Okay, follow me," he said as they made their way down the hall to the first examining room. He opened the door and let her into the well-stocked room first. Then he carefully helped her to climb onto the examining table before going to the sink to wash his hands. When he was done, he put on a white medical jacket that was hanging from a hook on the door, and then turned to her.

"Now that you know my name, why don't you tell me yours?"

"Regis Simpson. But people call me Reggie."

"Why?"

"Why what?"

"Why would people call you Reggie when Regis is such a pretty name?"

Her lips lifted to a sideward grin. "You've got one hell of a bedside manner, Doctor."

"Did it make you forget the throbbing in your leg?"

She thought a second and then chuckled softly. "That's *not* why you said that to me."

"Are you sure about that?" She was easy to tease, and Hawk quickly realized he liked this woman's spunk. But she was here for a reason, and once she was settled on the examining table, he immediately fell into professional mode.

"While I get what I need to clean your leg, why don't you tell me what happened?"

"I got into a fight with a rusty old fence on the other side of town and lost. I had to pull a piece out, but I don't think it's too bad. It just won't stop bleeding. I hope I didn't hit an artery."

Hawk looked up from the stainless steel tray he was putting gauze, saline solution and other supplies on. She was actually worried about it. "If you'd hit an artery you wouldn't have made it over here alive. You *are* bleeding a lot though, so let's have a look."

He pulled the table extender out and helped her lift her leg.

REGIS NEVER FELT SO foolish in her life. Handsome? Yeah, she couldn't deny that. But to ask her that? Was he full of himself of what? Never mind that she'd already been thinking that from the moment she'd seen him walking up the ramp.

"You didn't have a medical bag," she finally said.

He glanced at her. "Excuse me?"

"When you came up to the door you said the doctor does house calls in the middle of the afternoon. But you didn't have a medical bag so I naturally assumed ..."

His face suddenly showed understanding at her fumbled attempt at an explanation. "I keep the bag locked in the truck. You never know when you have to run out quickly, especially now." Turning his focus to her leg, he said, "I'm just going to pull your shoe and sock off so I can see how far down this cut went."

Regis looked above him, behind him and at the posters on the wall warning of germs and the importance of washing your hands as the doctor peeled off her blood-soaked sock and shoe. She closed her eyes to the pain as he turned her ankle.

"Let's clean out this wound and see how bad it is," he said. "Just lift your leg so I can put the towel underneath."

Gripping the table, she did as she was told and turned her head to the side as the cool liquid flowed over and stung her skin.

"You're not going to pass out on me, are you?"

"Not if I can help it."

"Nancy?" he called out, startling her.

A few seconds later, a middle-aged woman wearing a nurse's jacket with cats printed all over it was standing in the doorway.

"I wasn't sure you heard me come in," she said, looking over at Regis's leg and frowning. "Oh, you got yourself a nasty one there. Where'd that happen?"

Regis took a deep breath as the doctor worked on her leg. "Over at the Bennett property."

Sympathy showed on the woman's face. "I heard the whole first floor was flooded."

"It's about that bad," Regis said.

Hawk looked up at the nurse. "I didn't have time to fill out the paperwork for Miss—"

"Simpson. Regis Simpson," she said.

Hawk nodded. "Would you mind getting all that paperwork together while I take care of this wound?"

Nancy shook her head and frowned. But by the motherly look she gave Hawk, Regis knew she was teasing. "Didn't remember which form to fill out, huh? It's a good thing you're not at Sioux City General anymore. You think the other nurses would put up with this?"

"He didn't want me to bleed all over the new carpet."

Nancy chuckled with raised eyebrows. "That was very thoughtful of him. I see you already have this poor girl whipped. I'll get that paperwork."

As Nancy left, Hawk's hands paused on her leg as he looked up at her, giving her a wide smile that reached the depths of his eyes.

"You're getting me in trouble."

"I have a feeling you can do that all by yourself."

She wasn't sure what she'd been expecting from a country doctor, but the man standing next to her was not it. His eyes were the deepest shade of blue Regis had ever seen. He was tall, leanly muscled and had one of those ruggedly handsome faces that would've looked perfect in a cowboy movie. And she couldn't believe she was sitting on an examining table with the hots for her doctor.

Chapter Two

"IT'S REALLY NOT AS bad as it could have been," Hawk told her.

"How do you figure that when it hurts like hell?"

"You could have broken your leg. You'll have to be more careful out there and wear some sensible shoes. I've been out to the Bennett place since the floods came through. They still have a lot of debris to cleanup and it's tricky stepping."

"I found that out the hard way. I'm more ticked off about the ragged tear in my best pair of dress slacks than this puncture wound."

"Pants can be replaced. By the way, where did the name Regis come from?"

"My parents."

She tilted an eyebrow, and he wondered if it was in challenge or if she were teasing.

He hesitated a moment and then said, "What?"

"I'm just waiting for the standard comment about Regis being a boy's name, and oh, your father must have wanted a boy."

"Is that what everyone gives you? Standard lines?"

She shrugged as if she weren't uncomfortable with the topic. "I'm an insurance adjuster. Everyone wants to see me around here right now, and everyone is always giving me a line they hope will help their claim."

His lips lifted to a grin. "Then I won't make that mistake."

"I appreciate that," she said.

"So is it is true?"

"Is what true?"

"Did your father want a boy?"

Regis paused a fraction of a moment. "Yeah."

He'd hit a raw wound, and it wasn't the one on her leg. He let the name thing go and concentrated on her wounded ankle with gloved fingers gently probing at the damaged flesh. "You're not going to need stitches. But you may end up with a nasty scar."

She blew out a quick breath. "Good. I can add it to all the other ones I got as a kid."

"You're the insurance agent who denied the Proctor family's claim without even looking at the property."

Her sigh made him look up. A wry smile curved her lips. "Does that mean you're not going to treat me?"

Hawk chuckled as he stood. "If I didn't treat people who did things I didn't like, I wouldn't have much of a practice." He gathered a few items from a nearby cabinet and walked back over to her.

"I don't discuss my cases without my clients' permission."

"Evan Proctor said it was a technicality," he said as he began to clean out the wound. Her hands were gripping the edge of the table, but she didn't make a sound of pain, keeping her voice even. "Their policy had lapsed during the time frame of the flood."

"As I said, I don't discuss my cases without—"

"They're people. Not cases. These people lost their valuables, their homes and their livestock."

"I know that. That's why I'm doing everything I can to help them. But unfortunately, some things are beyond my control."

Hawk let the statement slide by, resisting the urge to tell her that there was always something that could be done. But it wasn't his job, and with the weight of the last few weeks bearing down on him, he realized he'd just crossed a very important line.

Once he'd finished cleaning her leg, he looked up at her. "Sorry, it's been a rough couple of weeks around here and many long days."

He'd expected annoyance, which was well earned for his transgression, and yet what he got from Regis Simpson was a sympathetic smile. That somehow made him feel worse.

"I know it's hard to see people you care about hurting. But it'll get better eventually," she said.

"That's what I'm hoping for."

"You asked about my name. Now it's your turn. What's the deal with Hawk?

"No deal. Just about everyone around here has known me since I was a kid, so everyone calls me Hawk."

"What's your name?"

"Didn't you read the sign?"

"There has to be a story that goes with Hawk. What is it about that name you don't like?"

"Nothing. My nephew is named Keith."

"Then why Hawk?"

The image of Wade flashed in his mind, and Hawk immediately felt that familiar pain he always felt when he thought of his older brother. "Your leg is wrapped. Make sure you keep it clean and dry tonight."

"Ah, you don't like talking about it?"

It was clear Regis knew she'd hit on something, but she didn't push further, and for that he was glad. She was new in town. She knew nothing of his family or of their personal tragedies. She dealt in tangible loss. And right now, a whole lot of people in Rudolph needed her help.

He pulled off his gloves and dropped them into the trash. "Are you staying at the motel in town?"

"You're changing the subject."

"I thought the subject was your wounded leg."

"What does my staying at the local motel have to do with my leg?"

From the little he'd seen of her, Regis Simpson was a pistol. And he liked that, Lord help him. He'd been with women in his life, and none of them challenged him. He wasn't a yes-dear man and he didn't want a yes-dear woman or someone who was only interested in being on the arm of a doctor and what his profession could provide. If he'd cared about any of that, he would have stayed in Sioux City instead of setting up his practice here in Rudolph where it was needed.

"You're going to need some antibiotic to help prevent a Staph infection. I have some antibiotic here, but it's not as strong as I'd like. I am going to call in a script to the pharmacy in the next county. They deliver, and I need an address for them to send it to you. Are there any meds you're allergic to?"

"Ah, no."

"Then I have enough for what you'll need tonight. I'll give you the pharmacy information so you can call and arrange for delivery."

"I can pick it up."

"No you won't. You need to stay off this leg. At least for the night. You need to give it time so it doesn't open up again. And you're going to need a tetanus shot."

"So I've heard."

Her reaction was instantaneous and amusing. He'd never seen an adult look so absolutely petrified at the mention of a shot.

He resisted the urge to laugh at the face she was making. "When was the last time you had a tetanus shot?"

She thought a moment, then shook her head without answering.

Frowning, he said, "Just as I thought. If you can't remember, it's been too long."

"I'm sure I've had one at some point. Maybe before college."

"And how long ago was that?"

"Eleven years."

"I'll finish bandaging your leg. Then we can see about doing that paperwork and getting you up to date on your shots. I'm surprised your boss doesn't require it given the work you do."

"Really, it's okay."

"No, it's not. You said the fence was rusty? Well, even if it's not, it's probably full of bacteria from the flood water. Do you have any idea what kind of pollutants flood waters carry? You don't want to take a chance—"

She started to protest, but he cut her off.

"And neither do I," he said. "It's your choice, but it's really for your own good, and I strongly advise you have it to prevent getting tetanus. Besides, there are too many people depending on you to do your job so they can get on with rebuilding. They'll be plenty mad at me if I don't take good care of you."

She bit her bottom lip until he thought she'd draw blood.

"Something wrong?"

"I don't like shots."

He scratched the back of his neck, fighting the smile pulling at his lips. "No one likes shots. But they're necessary. You had no problem driving here after pulling a hunk of metal out of your leg, but the thought of a shot scares you?"

She tried to glare at him, but the fear in her eyes drained all of the fire from it.

A wave of protectiveness washed over Hawk as he left the room to retrieve the syringe and vial of medicine from the locked cabinet. When he returned to the room, she was white-knuckling the edge of the table.

Tense was only part of what she was feeling. She looked terrified, and her response, given what she had to deal with on a daily basis, intrigued him. Hawk's eyes darted to Regis's pale face. She'd sunk her teeth into her bottom lip and was worrying at it again. He thought of her lips and how many times over the past fifteen minutes he'd thought about kissing them ... and hating himself for thinking that. Not here. Not like this. That's two transgressions in one day with the same woman.

He needed some sleep.

"Are you doing okay, Regis?" he asked.

"Please don't call me Regis."

"It's your name."

"Everyone calls me, Reggie. I never respond to Regis and have never been happy with that name. So, it's Reggie, okay?"

"Okay, Regis," he grinned at the flash of annoyance that cut through her fear. "I'm going to make this quick."

"I told you not to call me – ah!" The middle of her retort was cut off by a yelp as Hawk slid the needle into her arm. "What the hell, Hawk ... er, Dr. McKinnon," she growled.

He bit back a laugh. "If you prefer it, to be fair, you can call me Keith."

"I'm thinking of another name right now."

Then he did laugh. She was feisty for sure. And he liked that about her.

While he was sure she was a tough woman, he found her attempt at ferocity to be almost cute. Not that he was about to tell her that. He wasn't stupid. He dropped the syringe into the biohazard container on the floor.

"Are you going to be okay driving?" he asked.

"Sure."

He looked at her intently.

"What?"

"Your face has a little more color. For a while there, I thought you really were going to pass out."

He touched her arm to help her off the table. Her face flushed, and she pulled her arm away. "I'm fine."

"Good. Nancy has that paperwork for you to fill out before you leave."

"I know all about paperwork," she said, chuckling.

"I'm sure you do. I'll make that call to the pharmacy for you."

Hawk walked in the opposite direction that Regis went, and resisted the urge to turn back to look at her. For God's sake, she was a patient. She was here in town to help people he knew needed her to do her job so they could get on with their lives.

Yet, he didn't want to see her leave, and he definitely wanted to see Regis Simpson again. But not like this and not here. He'd fought the urge to ask her out for dinner. He'd find a moment that was right.

When he reached his office door, he turned around and caught her looking over her shoulder at him as she walked down the hall. He'd make that moment come very soon.

Fifteen minutes later, Hawk emerged from his office and walked to the front waiting area. Nancy was sitting behind the computer, inputting information from the paperwork Regis had just handed her. She lifted her eyes from Regis's paperwork only long enough to give him a teasing glance.

"Here is the name of the pharmacy," he said, handing Regis a piece of paper.

"Thank you, Keith."

He ignored the expression on his receptionist's face. Nancy had an opinion about everything, and he was sure he'd hear it once Regis left.

"Make sure you stay off that leg tonight. It's probably going to hurt a lot more once the adrenaline rush wears off."

"I will." Regis was out the door before Hawk could say anything more. And there were a whole lot of things spinning in his head that he wanted to ask her, starting with dinner, and where all that spunk he saw in her came from. He'd do that later.

He finally turned and stole a glance at Nancy.

"Keith?" she echoed.

"Breathe one word, and I'll tell everyone your middle name is Aggy."

Nancy gasped. "You wouldn't dare."

He smiled teasingly. "Only one way you'll find out."

Nancy rolled her eyes and went back to her typing as Hawk walked back to his office, unable to suppress his grin. He had some paperwork of his own to fill out for the Wounded Veterans Center if he was going to get out of here early. He had a house call to make tonight, and he didn't want to be late.

Chapter Three

MOTEL ROOMS HAD BEEN her home for far too long. Regis was so familiar with the blandness of each motel she stayed at that she never really paid attention to details. It only served to remind her about a childhood spending long periods of time in other people's homes on Army bases around the world while her dad was on tour somewhere else. At least now, she could be in the quiet of her own space without having to put on a smile for people she barely knew.

She'd managed to hobble her way out of the car and into her motel room and fire up her laptop so she could check which appointments she was going to miss the rest of the day. She'd have to switch around appointments tomorrow and bump a few to later in the week to keep her already heavy workload manageable. As soon as she'd figured out a workable plan, she called the homeowners who'd given her cell phone numbers with the news. Naturally, some were disappointed they'd have to wait another day or two for the inspections, and it meant she had to stay a little longer in Rudolph to get all her work done. But it couldn't be helped.

Dr. Keith McKinnon had been right about one thing, she felt the pain in her leg more now than she did when she'd initially fallen. With each movement on the bed, pain shot up her leg and brought tears to her eyes.

She finally closed the laptop and pushed it to the side of her bed, debating the need for getting up and grabbing the remote so she could watch television. Before boredom could win out, she heard a knock on the door and decided it must be the pharmacy delivering her prescription.

"Please let there be painkiller in there, too," she whispered. Then she called out, "Just a minute!"

Easing herself up off the bed, she limped to the door, being careful her sweatpants leg didn't fall over her bandage and cause the elastic to squeeze her leg. Even the slightest pressure was enough to send her through the roof. It was a struggle to get up on her tippy toes to look out of the peephole, but when she did, she stepped back, putting weight on her injured leg. Shooting pain nearly leveled her as she opened the door.

"I'd ask how you're doing, but from the look on your face, I'm guessing it's not so good."

Dr. Keith McKinnon stood outside the doorway looking better than he had earlier walking up the handicap ramp at his office. She, on the other hand, looked like road kill. She didn't have to look to know she had a serious case of bedhead from trying to take a nap earlier. Her old sweatpants and sweatshirt were comfy, but so big it made it hard to tell she was female underneath them.

She touched her hair just to make sure it wasn't sticking up. "What are you doing here?"

He lifted the white bag in his left hand. "Your prescription. When I called it into the pharmacy, they said they weren't making runs out this way due to all the flooding and roads being washed out."

She looked at the Styrofoam containers in his other hand. The glorious smell coming from them immediately made her stomach growl. "And what's that?"

"Dinner. For us. That is, if you're up for it."

She stepped aside to give Keith room to walk inside the motel room.

"Am I another house call?"

His voice was gentle as he spoke, making her head light. "No. But since you're from out of town, I knew you didn't have anyone else here to check on you, so I thought I'd make sure you were getting along. I figured you probably hadn't been able to grab a bite to eat yet either."

Warmth spread through her chest. "You wanted to check on me?"

"Sure." He lifted the containers. "Should I put these over on the table?"

She nodded; a sudden feeling of melancholy enveloping her. Keith didn't know how close to the truth he was. It had been a long time since there'd been anyone concerned with checking on her. In fact, she only spoke to her father about once a month because he was always so busy. The fact that Keith thought enough to stop by, and with dinner no less, was a first for her. She wasn't sure how to feel about it.

He was looking at her again.

"I'm not going to pass out," she said.

A low chuckle rumbled from his chest that Regis found enticing.

"No, but you do have this deer-in-the-headlights look about you."

"Do I?"

"Is something wrong? Did I come at a bad time?"

"No, it's just …" She didn't know exactly how to verbalize the oddness of having Dr. Keith McKinnon in her motel room.

Keith looked around the room, walking a few steps before he turned to her. "Looks okay to me. You didn't leave your dirty towel on the bathroom floor, did you?"

"Of course not. Besides the maid has been through the room today."

"Were you expecting someone else?"

"No. No, that's not it."

His brow narrowed. "Do I make you uncomfortable, Regis?"

Now there was a loaded question. The thing was, Dr. Keith McKinnon *did* make her uncomfortable. But for all the wrong reasons. Regis liked the way he looked at her. She liked the sound of his voice when he said her name. Her real name. She even liked the fact that he refused to call her by the nickname her dad had given her long ago, even though she'd repeatedly corrected him.

"I'm not used to having people in my motel room. It's usually … just my own quiet space."

His dark eyebrows lifted. "Never?"

She shook her head. "I visit ten to fifteen different cities and towns a year. This is a first."

His lips lifted on one side in a way that Regis could only call sexy. The warm feeling in her chest grew.

"I like that. Being a first. But if you would prefer I leave, I will. I don't want you to be uncomfortable."

"I'm not uncomfortable," she said quietly. "You brought me dinner. The least I can do is offer you a seat at my table to enjoy it." She looked back at the small desk and realized there was only one chair. "You can take the chair at the desk, and I'll sit on the bed."

"Good choice. You need to keep your leg elevated."

She hobbled over to the bed and eased down on it while Keith carried the food to the desk.

"I have some sodas in the mini-fridge."

Keith went to the mini-fridge by the dresser and pulled out two cans of soda. "Want a glass?"

"No, it's just one more thing to clean."

He put the cold soda on the nightstand next to her and then handed her one of the Styrofoam containers with a set of plastic utensils and a napkin.

"I thought the diner was closed this time of the night," she said, lifting the lid and fully breathing in the aroma of good home cooking.

"It is. My mother is working down at the shelter again. It's actually the elementary school, but for now it's a working shelter. At least, it's been for the last couple of weeks. Tomorrow everyone should be in temporary housing while they rebuild."

"Your mother owns the diner?"

He smiled with pride. "Since before I was born. Every single one of us McKinnons took our first steps across that dining room floor. Although my mother will swear we all never walked, we just ran."

Regis smiled picturing it. "How many McKinnons are there?"

"Five boys."

She dropped the fork full of food in the container. "Five? Your mother ran a diner and raised five boys at the same time?"

"Amazing, huh?" he said with pride.

They both took a bite of food and were quiet for a few moments. Regis had eaten out of many a Styrofoam container over the years, but there was nothing like home cooking.

"So what about you?" Keith finally asked.

"What about me?"

"Where are you from?"

"Everywhere."

He frowned. "No one place to call home?"

Regis lifted a shoulder. "I'm an Army brat. I've lived on bases all over the world."

"Wow. That must have been quite an adventure for your parents and you."

"Just my dad and me," she said. "My mom didn't like the Army life. Or family life for that matter. She took off when I was six. It was just my dad and me after that. Just me when he was on tour."

He looked shocked, like most people did when she said that. "Who'd take care of you when your father was gone?"

"I usually got placed with another family on base ... or two or three while my father was gone. Homecomings were better than times he shipped out. Most families were going through their own trials with a parent gone. It was hard taking care of a snotty kid like me who didn't exactly want to be with them any more than they wanted me to be there."

"You? Snotty?"

"I was a kid. Aren't all kids snotty when they're missing their dad?"

"You have a point. That must have been rough on you though."

"Like anything else, you learn to adapt. At least it made acclimating to my present job easier, since I'm always on the road."

"So where's home?"

She shrugged. "Here right now. Next month, who knows?"

"You're a gypsy."

His voice was as smooth as silk when he said the words, almost as if he liked the intrigue of it.

"I guess you could say that. Except I'm not going to tell your fortune or dance for you."

He raised his eyebrows with a wicked grin. "Now that sounds very enticing. I wouldn't mind seeing you in silk and gems."

Warmth flowed through her as the heat in Keith's eyes flared.

"Do you talk this way to all of your patients, Dr. McKinnon?"

"Hawk."

"I thought you said I could call you Keith?"

His lips tilted to a slight grin, then looked at the container sitting on her lap. "Your dinner is getting cold."

AFTER DINNER, KEITH checked the bandage on Regis's leg.

"Make sure you keep this dry for at least another day. As long as you can walk on it without pain, you can get around.

But keep your activity down to a minimum or you'll risk opening up the wound again."

"No can do. I already had to cancel a long list of appointments today. Now I have an even longer list of properties to see tomorrow."

"I talked with my cousin, Ian, earlier. He mentioned you'd called him about rescheduling your inspection of the Center."

She frowned. "Center?"

"It's the old mill by the river. It was being converted to a community center, but there's space for the Wounded Veterans Center there as well as its other functions. Ian is a wounded veteran. My brother, Ethan, is a retired Navy Seal. They've been working to get the old mill transformed into a center for the vets in the area as well as have it funded by regular functions. Dances and weddings and such. My younger brother Logan and his fiancé are hoping to be the first to have their wedding there. It's a pretty spot. Or at least, it was before the floodwaters came in."

"Oh, that's right. I'm sorry. I talked with a lot of people today. I do remember talking to a man named Ian. I didn't make the connection."

"There are quite a few of us in these parts."

"I guess so. I look forward to meeting them while I'm here."

He nodded. "I would like to see you again."

"I don't think I'll really need a follow-up appointment for this. I should be able to wrap this myself now that I've seen you do it twice already." She reached for her cell phone so she could check her calendar. "To be quite honest, I don't think I could fit—"

"I wasn't thinking of an office visit. I was thinking more alone the lines of having dinner again."

She eased the cell phone back into place on the night table. "Excuse me?"

"I enjoyed being with you tonight. I thought you might like a repeat."

THE DEER-IN-THE-HEADLIGHTS expression was back on her face, Hawk realized. Regis was staring at him, wide-eyed with her lips slightly parted. He waited for her to respond, but he wasn't altogether sure she was even breathing until she finally spoke.

"I don't like to get ... involved," she said.

"You're never in one place long enough for that, are you?"

"No."

"You eat alone every night?"

"Most of the time, yes. Sometimes I have dinner with one of my colleagues if they're in the same town, but most of the time we're all too exhausted and have too much paperwork to do."

"Sounds lonely."

"It's the nature of the beast."

"It doesn't have to be. Especially when someone is offering you a home cooked meal."

Her mouth dropped open. "Home cooked?"

"Yeah, my house. Okay,

"Your house."

"Well, not exactly home cooked like my mother's. But I have a pizza stone that needs breaking in. We can be creative."

She shook her head. "I ... when I'm on the job, things get complicated."

"You don't like complicated?"

She sighed slowly, seeming to choose her words carefully. "Sometimes I have to deliver bad news, like with the Proctors. I hate it. It's the worst part of my job. But it's a fact. It makes things easier if I just keep to myself."

A grin tugged at his mouth. "I didn't propose marriage, Regis. Just pizza." He kept his tone matter-of-fact, trying to ignore just how badly he wanted her to say yes. He'd been watching her all night, wondering if the intrigue he'd felt earlier in the day would be gone. She'd greeted him with messy hair, make-up smeared down her cheek, and old gray sweats that were probably two sizes too big and still she looked like the sexiest thing he'd ever seen. He looked at that cluster of freckles on her cheek and wanted to rub his thumb across it as he looked into her eyes.

Hawk watched the choices play across her face. But then she was shaking her head again. "Thank you for the offer, but I have to decline. And thank you for this tonight. I was wondering if I was going to get to eat more than just Cheetos and peanuts from the vending machine outside."

He forced a smile he didn't feel. "Well, I'm glad we had the chance to talk tonight then."

She started to get up off the bed, but he held her back with his hand.

"I'll let myself out. You stay off your leg at least for tonight. Make sure you come back to the office if your leg gives you trouble."

Hawk had his hand on the doorknob when Regis stopped him.

"Thank you for tonight. I'm not ... I don't usually have to depend on people. I'm glad you stopped by."

"It was my pleasure."

Hawk whistled as he left Regis's room and made his way to his truck in the motel parking lot. She'd turned him down, but he could see that she was conflicted. To him, that just meant he'd have to win her over another way. One thing was for sure, he was more intrigued with Regis Simpson than he was when he'd arrived tonight. And that only made him want to see her more. And he would. He was sure of it.

He slammed the truck door closed and turned the key in the ignition, whistling while the engine fired to life. He couldn't recall the last time he'd whistled.

Chapter Four

HER LEG WAS BLEEDING again. It wasn't even noon, and she'd already managed to get off schedule after brushing up against the fender of her car while taking pictures of a house with roof damage. It should have been a quick appointment, lasting no more than ten minutes to talk to the owner and take pictures. Instead, she needed mending. Again.

Disgusted with herself, Regis pulled her sedan into the clinic parking lot. She killed the engine and drummed her fingers on the steering wheel. She should have gone back to her hotel and just patched her leg up herself. But …

But she was here at the clinic to see Dr. Keith McKinnon again. Yeah, the reason for that wasn't too big of a mind stretch for her. She'd thought of nothing but him since he'd shown up at her motel room last night.

What the hell was she doing? He'd asked her to dinner. And she'd emphatically said no. She never dated men while on the road. They'd get attached. She'd get attached. And then she'd move on to another town. That was the story of her childhood. She didn't want to repeat it in her adult life.

Besides, long distance relationships never worked. She'd learned that one the hard way when she'd held on too long.

"And this is not a date," she muttered, opening the car door. "I'm only here to have my leg wrapped again and then I'll be back on the road."

Oh, why couldn't Keith McKinnon be a crusty old doctor? Instead, she couldn't stop thinking about the drop-dead gorgeous country doctor with a heart of gold she'd only seen in heroes in movies.

Ten minutes later, she was sitting on the same examining table she'd sat on the day before, looking into those deep blue eyes that had haunted her all last night. He'd dispensed with wearing the white jacket he'd put on yesterday, making it hard to see him as the caring doctor he'd been. Instead, strong muscles were clearly visible beneath the fabric of his long sleeved gray shirt. The blue jeans he wore were faded and had stains that clearly had defied laundering.

"Am I keeping you from something?" she asked.

"You just caught me. I was heading over to the mill to help with some of the cleanup."

She nodded. "That's another thing on my list that I'm going to have to reschedule. Again."

Regis fought the tears of frustration she'd been feeling since yesterday's mishap. So many people were counting on her, and she was failing.

"Come on. It's not that bad," Keith said, lifting her chin with his finger. The sympathy she saw in his eyes was more than she could take. She lost the battle with her emotions as the tears she'd been holding back fell down her cheek.

Reaching behind him, Keith grabbed a tissue box and held it out for her. She took two and nodded her thanks.

"I'm so embarrassed," she finally said when she got her emotions in check. "I don't normally blubber like this."

"Why not? It looks like you were overdue."

She shook her head. "I can hear my father in my head tell me to buck up. 'Soldiers don't cry.'" She lowered her voice in that deep way she always did when she mimicked her father's admonition. She hadn't done that in a long time.

"You were a soldier?"

"No, my dad is."

"Oh."

His sudden silence had her looking up at Keith. "What?"

He shrugged as he grabbed a fresh roll of gauze from the cabinet. "I don't know your father, but I do know a lot of people in the military. Male or female, they do cry. How could they not? And plenty of people cry with them. There's nothing wrong with some tears."

His kind words only made Regis feel worse and her tears renewed.

"I can't do what I have to do with this leg."

"The longer you stay off it, the better chance the wound has to heal and stay closed.

"I can't stay off my feet long enough for this to heal."

"You don't have sick time from work?"

"It's not that. I'm sure I can call my office, and they'll send another adjuster out here to replace me. But ..."

He cocked his head slightly to one side and waited for her to go on.

"I've been at this a long time," she said. "There are a lot of people who do what I do who aren't thorough."

She glanced up at him, hoping he'd get her meaning. After a second, he nodded.

"It's very noble to be conscientious about your job. In fact, that's something I got from you immediately. You care about what you do. I'm sure not everyone would be as dedicated."

"Thank you. I just want to make sure these people get what they need first." She took a deep breath and used the tissues to wipe her cheeks. "So what's the prognosis? Am I back in the saddle when you get me patched up?"

His slow sigh gave her the answer. "If you want this leg to heal so you can really get around the way you need to, you're going to need to stay off it for at least another day."

"That's not poss—"

"Or every time you bend your foot or rub up against something, you risk re-injuring yourself."

"So warned."

He finished inspecting her leg and then wrapped it up. He dropped his latex gloves in the trash and turned to her.

"Who do you have on your list today?"

"My schedule is in the car."

"Then let's take a look."

Fifteen minutes later they were standing in the clinic parking lot. Regis pulled her tablet from the car and was now scrolling down the list of names of people she'd need to contact.

Keith was standing incredibly close to her. She felt the heat of his body as it shielded her from the March wind, and the light smell of aftershave. She hadn't noticed it earlier, but that was the difference about him today. She'd noticed the light scruff of hair on his jawline yesterday, but now it was cleanly shaven. Just standing so close to him made her head light, making it hard to concentrate.

"You were going to go to the mill today," he said, seemingly unaware of his effect on her.

"That was the plan." The wind whipped her hair around her face. She fought with trying to keep it from obstructing her vision for a few seconds. When it subsided, she noticed Keith was staring intently at her list.

"Okay, then," he said, moving away from her and leaving her in the wind. He opened her driver's side door and reached inside the car, pulling out her camera.

"Okay then what?" she asked.

"We'll take my truck. This is the only camera you use?"

Confused, she said, "Yes. But don't you have appointments?"

"I had them all this morning. I was just about to leave when you came in."

"Doesn't anyone else besides me need a doctor around here?" she said, chuckling.

Keith laughed too, and the sound of it made her smile. Not just a smile on her face, but a smile she felt inside. Good Lord, when was the last time any man had made her feel that way? Ever!

"Hopefully not for the rest of the day. That way we can get through the list."

"You're going to come with me?"

"Yes. If it means you're not going to hurt yourself again. Look, I know the area better than you. I also know the terrain. If there is any place that is too difficult to walk on or can cause you injury, I'll go and take the pictures. Then you won't get too far behind."

She looked up at the strong features of his face, scrutinized the blue eyes she couldn't stop thinking about, just to see if he was kidding. He was serious.

"Why are you doing this?" she asked quietly.

"Why not?"

"You just met me. You don't even really know me."

He nodded and pointed out into the distance. "But I know them. And I do know that doing this right is important to you. So I figure the best way for me to help people I know and care about is to help you. It's a win-win situation. Is there anything wrong with that?"

She drew in a slow breath, unable to find words of gratitude that seemed genuine.

"Thank you," was all she managed.

THE TRUCK SMELLED LIKE Regis. They'd been to three properties already on their way to the mill and each time Hawk climbed into the truck, the scent of her filled his head.

"Right over there is the Maitland ranch. That's where I got on my first bull."

Regis gave him a quick glance. "You were a bull rider?"

"I didn't say that. I got on the bull, and it immediately bucked me off. I don't even think I lasted a second. But I did give it a second and third try, mostly because my brother, Wade, dared me to."

"Wade?"

He caught himself. It wasn't often he talked about Wade. And it occurred to him that Wade probably would've been angry at him for closing himself off that way. But even after nearly five years, losing his brother still felt as raw as it did the day they got the news.

"My oldest brother. He's first, then me, then Sam, then the twins, Ethan and Logan." He drove in silence for a few seconds, allowing himself to think about things he hadn't thought of for a long time. "Wade was good at bull riding. He was never serious enough to go pro, but he had no fear of that bull."

Regis smiled at him. "You admired him a lot."

Hawk nodded. "He was the best friend I've ever had." And Hawk had let him down.

His hand went to his chest to feel the small medallion and chain that Wade always wore from the time he was a teenager until before he'd gone on that trip with the Peace Corps that last time.

"I'm an only child," Regis said. "I can't even imagine what it would have been like to grow up with a houseful of boys like you all did. You must have driven your parents crazy."

"We're McKinnons," he said laughing. "I can't imagine what it would have been like growing up without noise and chaos. My parents seemed to thrive on it. You said you lived on military bases growing up. What was that like?"

She shrugged. "Different." She turned her head to look at the side of the road. Hawk didn't push it.

"Did you go to this high school?" she asked as they passed the school.

"Yes. On really hot days in the spring, Sam and I used to skip class and head down to the pond on through the woods with some of the other kids in school. Denny's house was out there." He pointed to a long driveway that disappeared into the woods. "Denny was really Ethan's friend, but we all hung out. And we always got caught when we did."

Laughing, Regis asked, "By who?"

"My dad mostly. And believe me, he wasn't too happy about it. But when the principal would call him at the drilling company and tell him that four of his boys had suddenly disappeared from the school, he wanted to take care of things in person, especially since he knew my mom couldn't leave the diner during the day back then. She has a lot more help running the diner now. But my dad always knew where to find us."

"Drilling company. You mean, as in MW Oil? That big plant I saw a few towns back when I came into Rudolph?"

"That's the one. Started by my father's grandparents and passed down the line."

"Did any of you boys join the family business?"

He made a face and looked at her.

Her beautiful eyes widened. "No?"

"Dad gave up hoping long ago and is now trying to convince my four-year-old nephew that it's up to him."

"No pressure though," she said, with a giggle.

Regis looked on her tablet at the list of properties she had to inspect.

"Do you have the Coleman property on the list?" Hawk asked.

"Yes, but not for today."

"Good."

She gave him a questioning look.

"Bob Coleman isn't always happy to see me."

"Why?"

"I'm not sure he's ever forgiven me for driving his tractor into the side of his barn."

"What?

"Don't listen to any stories about it either. I swear it was a faulty brake. I didn't do it on purpose."

"Were you and your brothers always trouble?"

He chuckled with the memory. "Let's just say people in town knew the name McKinnon. It's a good thing they all loved my mom."

Regis's chuckle turned into a full-blown laugh, and Hawk decided that he'd found his new favorite sound. He wanted to hear it more. But then it changed, and she was quiet again.

"I envy you knowing so much about where you live. Knowing everyone. I barely remember some of the names of people I lived with."

"How many did you live with?"

She drew in a deep breath. "Too many. Every time my father had to leave, I got placed with a new family on base to stay with. It was a lot like living in a foster home, I suppose."

He nodded as if he understood, and yet, Hawk couldn't imagine a life like that.

Since the sun would be setting in an hour, they decided to head over to the mill to inspect the property. Regis had called Ian, but got no answer, so Hawk called his brother Ethan, who agreed to meet them. Ethan's police SUV was parked on the muddied road, and he was standing outside.

"You made it," he said as Hawk parked his truck. "I was worried I'd get a call and have to take off before you got here."

"We got hung up at the Jordan property," Hawk said, getting out of the car.

Regis got out of the truck and limped over to where Ethan and Hawk were standing. Hawk could see that the busy day had taken its toll on her, and she was fading fast.

"Ethan, this is—"

"Reggie Simpson," Ethan said. "We met a few days ago at the diner."

"How are you doing? I didn't realize you were Keith's brother."

Ethan raised his eyebrows. "Keith?"

Hawk shot his brother a warning glare, which earned him a laugh from Ethan. But instead of the normal ribbing he would have gotten, Ethan turned his attention to Regis.

"Keith tells me you were a Navy Seal."

Ethan smiled with pride as he looked at the weathered red façade of the Buxton Mill. "Yes, ma'am. That's why this place is so important."

"Well, let's take a look and see what the damage is."

The terrain was rough on the exterior of the mill. Hawk extended his hand to Regis to give her support as she walked.

"I'm fine," she said in a quiet voice when they got to the stairs by the door. His hand lingered, linked with hers for longer than he needed. But Hawk was in no hurry to let go until Regis pulled away.

"I heard Poppy and Mom talking about a winter wedding here. Seems Poppy has her heart set on having the ceremony in the back by the floor to ceiling windows overlooking the river," Ethan said.

"Winter weather is unpredictable, but it'll be a pretty spot if it snows."

Regis looked around the room. "But there are no floor to ceiling windows here."

"It's all in the new plans that Ian drew up for the place. He's put a lot of time and money into the design and use for the property and has worked with the building commissioner to make sure we can get the permits to get this dream realized."

They walked through the main floor of the Buxton Mill while Hawk and Ethan described the plans for the center. Every so often, Regis snapped pictures with her camera and made notes on her tablet.

"How did you happen to come across this property for a community center?" Regis asked.

"It was a small, family owned business for over a hundred years until about fifteen years ago when the oldest family member died, and the company got squeezed out by the bigger mills in the state. The others were retiring and didn't have a buyer who was interested in doing anything, but tearing it down and putting up condos because of the river location," Ethan explained. "The Buxtons were a family of veterans that went all the way back to World War I and decided they wanted to donate the property to the town for a community center as long as we established space in it for the Wounded Veterans Center."

"That was generous of them," Regis said, stepping back and taking another few pictures as she listened.

"Well, there was back taxes and debt to pay, but we managed to raise the money locally for that," Ethan added. "Ian has been instrumental in working the cause. I think it saved him, to be honest."

Regis lowered the camera and looked at both of them. "Saved him?"

Hawk thought of his cousin and how far he'd come. "He was a mess when he came back from Iraq. But this has given him a reason to get out of bed, and for that alone, I'm grateful to the Buxtons for their gift. Now we just have to get this place up to speed."

They finished their tour of the mill, which took longer than the other properties because of its size and proximity to the river. Just as they were wrapping up, Ethan got a call over the police radio.

"I have a call down at the high school," Ethan said. "I've got to run."

"Are you going to stop in and see Maddie?"

Ethan made a face that gave him his answer.

"She's got to talk to you sometime."

He shook his head. "No she doesn't," he said quietly. To Regis, he added, "Do you need anything else?"

"We're all set here," Regis said. "Thank you for meeting with me."

"No problem. You know where to find me if you have any questions. And you have Ian's number. I'm sure he can answer more than I can. He would have been here today but ..."

"I understand. It was last minute so I appreciate you taking the time."

A few minutes later, Ethan was pulling out of the parking lot in his SUV, and the two of them were alone at the empty mill. They were losing light fast, and the ground was disappearing in the darkness as they walked back to the truck, making it hard to see the ruts in the dried mud. Knowing Regis was already tired, and not wanting her to injure herself again, Hawk took matters into his own hands. In one fell swoop, he scooped Regis up into his arms.

Chapter Five

THE LAST THING REGIS had expected when she'd agreed to have Hawk help her today was ending up in his arms. When he'd put a strong arm behind her knees and the other around her waist, she was in the air instantly. His jacket was open, and she was pressed up against his rock hard chest before she could say a word of protest.

"Don't argue," he said. His face was just inches from hers as he carried her effortlessly across the parking lot to the truck.

"This isn't necessary."

"It's just insurance that you don't get hurt again and wind up on my examining room table. I'd much rather see you outside my office than in it."

When they reached the truck, Hawk stood next to the passenger side door and held Regis in his arms, just looking at her. She could feel his warmth, see the mist of his breath against the cold air, and feel his heart beating against her.

"You can put me down now," she said, her heart beating wildly in her chest.

"I don't think so."

"What?"

"I like you right where you are."

"Please put me down, Keith," she said quietly.

His lips lifted to a half grin. "I really like it when you say my name."

"I thought you didn't like people calling you by your given name."

"I like the way you say it. In fact, I like it a lot."

"You do?"

He had a full-blown smile now. "I like you a lot."

"Keith?"

"What?"

"Please put me down."

"I kind of like having you right here in my arms."

She drew in a deep breath. "You don't like me. You only think you like me. You don't even know me."

He chuckled against her eye and whispered, "Then let's get to know each other."

She turned away from him, feeling her resolve wither away. "I don't like to get involved—"

"You don't like complicated. Well, I mean to change that."

He slowly lowered her so her feet were on the ground, but he kept his arm around her and pulled her closer with the other arm.

"I want to kiss you."

"Are you always this direct?"

With his hand, he pushed aside the hair the wind blew in her face, and bent his head so that his mouth was only inches from hers. "Only when I want something very badly."

And then his warm mouth was against hers, and to her surprise, Regis didn't protest. Instead, she melted into the warmth that Keith provided, both in body and spirit. His hands were in her hair, pulling her closer as his mouth devoured hers. And she gave back what was given and wanted more.

She couldn't remember the last time she'd felt so completely undone by a man with just a touch or a look or a kiss. Keith's kisses weren't anything like she'd felt before. He wasn't a man like anyone she'd ever known before.

And it scared her to death and excited every single bit of her at the same time.

He pulled away slowly, with his mouth still just inches from hers.

"I could use a whole lot more of these," he said. Even as the night grew darker, she could see his lips curled into a pleasing smile.

"I don't think that was such a hot idea."

"Regis, I'm plenty hot right now, and I think the idea of kissing the woman who got me there is just fine."

She drew in a slow breath and took a step back, out of his arms. And he let her. He didn't try to keep her where she didn't want to be. Except, she'd liked it a whole lot better when Keith's arms were wrapped around her. And that was just the problem.

"What do you want from me, Keith? This can't go anywhere good."

She couldn't see his eyes or his expression in the darkness, but she could see his frown.

"I don't have a crystal ball. But I do know that I like you. And that hasn't happened for me in a very long time."

Her heart melted with his words. It was as if he were reading her mind.

"I know the feeling."

"Then don't we owe it to ourselves to at least find out what this is?"

Regis had a feeling she'd regret any answer she gave him.

"IT'S ONLY DINNER," she mumbled to herself as she drove to the clinic. Regis had managed to get some sleep, and work a full day setting up her space on a table in the large meeting room at the Senior Center next to the FEMA representatives and a number of other insurance adjusters who were in town to help. Despite having a full day of work, she was surprisingly energetic and decided all this energy was the lingering adrenaline rush after the kiss three days ago.

She still couldn't believe she'd kissed Keith. And then actually agreed to have dinner with him tonight, breaking the first rule of being on the road. Of course, he was probably the most persistent man she'd ever met. In the days since they'd kissed at the mill, Keith had made it a point to stop by and see her at the motel to check on her. He never stayed long. He didn't talk about the kiss they'd shared. He just spent time with her and then always asked her to dinner. And she'd always say no. Until last night.

She liked him. Regis couldn't deny it. And he said he felt the same way about her. In fact, Regis really liked the way Keith was not at all shy about admitting his feelings. She'd never been that open with a man before. And while it caught her off guard ... she liked it.

"You're such an idiot, Reggie," she mumbled as she pulled into the parking lot of the clinic next to his truck. Disgusted with herself, she killed the engine and sat in the car looking at the clinic. The light was on inside, and she could see through the window that Nancy was standing inside the waiting room talking to someone. She had her heavy winter coat wrapped around her and her purse hiked up on her shoulder.

"It's just pizza. Even you can handle that." Even as she tried to downplay the importance of this dinner, Regis struggled with the idea of actually going through with it. Still, her palms were sweaty, and her heart was pounding through her chest as she pushed the car door open.

She checked her reflection in the mirror for the umpteenth time since she'd left the motel, unable to stop thinking about the man she was going to meet. It wasn't just that Keith McKinnon was incredibly handsome. He was, and what was so charming was that, despite him teasing her about it the day they met, he didn't seem to realize just how handsome he was. But she had met plenty of good-looking men over the years. The bases she'd lived on all over the world had provided lots of teenage crushes, and one hell of a heartbreak that was difficult to think about even now.

But none of them had ever stuck in her mind the way Keith McKinnon had. There was just something about the man that had kept her awake last night. And it wasn't just the constant replay of the kiss at the mill the other day. It would have been easy to blame her sleepless night on pain in her leg. But that hadn't been the source of her restlessness last night. And as Keith had predicted, her leg was feeling a whole lot better today, to the point where she hardly noticed it at all.

Days ago she'd seen him pull into the parking lot and walk up the ramp toward her. It shouldn't have been a big deal, but the memory made her flush with heat. Just remembering the look on his face and the way she'd reacted ... she'd made a fool of herself. And after her reaction to his kiss, she was convinced she was still making a fool of herself.

Regis walked up the ramp until she reached the landing, and then pushed the door open. The warm air from the office hit her in the face as she stepped inside.

Nancy smiled knowingly when she saw her. "There's the girl of the hour."

"Excuse me?"

"Never mind," Keith said. "Nancy was just on her way out."

"Am I late?"

Nancy chuckled. "Depends on whose clock you're looking at. How's that leg?"

"Hasn't fallen off yet."

Nancy laughed harder. "Sense of humor is there? That's always a good sign." She touched Regis on the shoulder as she passed to the door. "Enjoy your evening."

Regis waited for Nancy to step outside before turning to Keith.

"What was that all about?"

"Nothing. Nancy is a good friend of my mother's and the two of them have been trying to get me married off since I was twelve. They're hoping some nice girl will tame me."

"Is that so?"

"That seems to be the plan."

"But you're against the idea. Marriage that is."

He thought about it a second. "No. I just don't believe in putting the cart before the horse. I don't want to get married just to get married."

"That's a recipe for disaster for everyone left behind."

He stopped what he was doing mid-motion. "Sounds like you're talking from personal experience."

She hadn't realized she'd said that last part out loud. "You promised me homemade pizza," she said, changing the subject.

He frowned, and her stomach fell. "I did. But we may have a problem."

"After all your convincing for me to come to dinner, you're backing out?"

"Not a chance. But apparently a pipe burst at the school they're using as an emergency shelter, and while a lot of the displaced people have temporary housing, there are still people there, and they need to be fed."

She looked out the window and saw the diner lights on and the parking lot full of cars. "The diner looks packed."

"Yeah, but the diner isn't big enough to handle it all. Mom said they needed a place for overflow, and the only place big enough to handle it that was close enough to the diner is my place. So my kitchen is in full use. There are a lot of hands helping out tonight."

"We don't have to do this tonight," she said.

He gave her an irresistible half grin. "You're not getting out of this that easy. Ethan called a little while ago and said they're packaging everything up now. All I can say is that I can't vouch for the state of my kitchen until I get there, so consider yourself forewarned."

"Let's go see the damage then."

KEITH INSISTED SHE drive with him to the house and leave her car in the clinic's parking lot. He was probably afraid she'd bolt when she saw all the cars lined up his driveway.

"Looks like half the town is here," she said.

He chuckled as he pushed the truck door open. "No, just mostly McKinnons and other volunteers that have been helping out since the flood."

"Just a dinner," she muttered as she pushed the car door open.

"What?"

"Nothing."

She ran her fingers through her hair and climbed out of his truck, thankful she'd changed out of her work clothes into a comfortable pair of jeans and a black peasant top. Her leg didn't hurt as much as it did, but she still chose a pair of black running shoes over a dressier high-heeled boot to be on the safe side.

She'd only gone a few steps when a dark-haired man bearing a striking resemblance to Keith came out of the house with a large box in his arms.

He smiled at Keith as they approached.

"I should have known you'd show up just as all the work is finished," he said.

Keith spread his hands as if defeated. "You think I'm stupid? What is the state of my kitchen?"

"It's still there." The man looked at Regis, then at Keith, and then back at Regis. "I'd shake your hand, but they're full. I'm Logan. If I wait for my idiot brother to introduce me, these dinners will spoil. And they're getting heavy."

As if just catching himself, Keith shook his head. "Sorry. Regis Simpson, this is my smart-assed brother. He actually thinks he needs to keep me in line."

"That must come from somewhere," Regis said, smiling at Logan.

Logan laughed, gave Keith a teasing look, and then he eased the box into the back of a truck that already had a few boxes filled with containers. "She's smart. I'd keep her close if I were you."

The screen door to the log cabin opened, and a tall woman walked onto the porch holding a little boy's hand.

"Don't leave without us, Daddy!" the little boy called out as if he were worried about being left behind.

"No worries, little man. I need you to help me carry all this food."

Keith turned to Regis. "This little man about to tackle me is my nephew, Keith." He bent down to pick the little boy up as he launched into his arms, giggling. The bond between the two was evident by the way they connected so lovingly.

"You know, I'm standing here, too," the woman said.

"Sorry, Poppy."

Logan laughed. "Usually I'm getting in trouble for failed introductions. Regis, this is my soon-to-be bride, Poppy Ericksen."

"Not soon enough for me," Poppy said, gazing at Logan with a twinkle in her eye. Regis found herself fighting off the stab of envy in her stomach. They all seemed so close, something she'd never experienced in her lifetime.

"Nice to meet you."

"Ethan told me you were out at the mill assessing the damage," Poppy said.

Regis nodded. "We were there the other day."

"Good. The sooner they get all their paperwork done for the claim, the sooner they can get all the estimates for renovations, and they can start building. I have my heart set on a winter wedding there at the end of the year."

"Congratulations," Regis said. "It looks like it will be a pretty spot."

"Thank you. That's what we're hoping," Logan said, scooping Poppy by the waist and pulling her close to him. "We need to get this food over to the school so they can start feeding people."

Keith glanced into the back of the truck. "Looks like you've got a full load. That's good."

"Ethan already took off with a bunch of boxes. He's waiting for us at the school," Poppy said. She kissed Keith on the cheek and said, "Make sure you ask your mother why she can't stop smiling."

He looked at Poppy, then quickly looked at Logan. " It's too soon for you ..."

"To be expecting? Jeez, give us a little time why don't you," Poppy said, chuckling as she shook her head.

"Then what is it?"

Logan took his son in his arms and carried him over to the open truck door to help him into his car seat. "Ask Mom."

They said their good-byes as they walked to the log home. As the pick-up rumbled away, Keith led Regis up the stairs just as the door opened again. A man and woman emerged, carrying the same type of containers Keith's brother had. The woman gave them a half-smile that spoke of long days and fatigue. Regis hoped she wasn't someone whose claim she had to investigate. But in all likelihood, she either had already or her name was on a long list of people she needed to visit.

It wasn't until Keith started to introduce them that Regis remembered they'd already met.

Chapter Six

"REGIS, I'D LIKE TO introduce you to—"

"Ali Hubbard," she finished for him, feeling relief wash over her with the memory. "I was out to see you last week."

"I wondered if you'd remember," Ali said. "All our faces and names must blend together after a while."

"Sometimes it feels that way. But I pay close attention and take great notes to make sure I don't miss anything."

Yes, she *did* remember the details. Ali and James Hubbard. Ten acres on the outskirts of town. Lost half of their livestock and their barn. Regis had approved the claim her first day in town and submitted the paperwork to the insurance company. She was now waiting for their final payout decision.

She let out an easy breath with the recollection. The claims that were seamless didn't stress her out. The denied claims were the worst, and the reason she liked to get into a town, do her job, and get out without any complication. The denied claims broke her heart, but not nearly as much as it did the homeowners. She had to focus on the ones she could help.

Keith held open the door, and they both slipped inside. She stood for a moment, overwhelmed by all the activity around her. It was as if Keith had planned a party especially for her. The room was filled with people of all ages. Some she recognized from when she ate at the diner. Some were people she didn't know. Some she could tell definitely had McKinnon blood in them just by their strong resemblance to each other. To her relief, all of them were too busy putting filled containers of food into bigger boxes to notice her.

She followed Keith through the living room to the kitchen. At the oven was an older woman wearing a blue and white checkered apron and matching oven mitts. Her salt and pepper hair was cut short, framing an oval face that was pleasant and familiar.

"Ah, you made it!" the woman said with a warm smile. "Don't worry, we'll be cleaned up in about 10 minutes. All the meals are being served over at the school. I just need to wrap up the left overs and bring them over to the diner's freezer."

"Mom," Keith addressed the woman in the apron and bent his head to give her a kiss, which she warmly accepted. "I want you to meet ..."

"Reggie Simpson," the woman said, finishing his sentence.

Keith's eyes narrowed as he glanced back at her.

Regis smiled. "I told you everyone calls me Reggie. It's nice to see you again, Mrs. McKinnon."

His mother turned to Keith and gave her son an insulted look. "I may be a little absent-minded at times when it comes to where I put my car keys, but I'm not about to forget someone I've fed breakfast to for the past four days." With a wink, she said, "You can call me Kate."

Regis's greeting was sincere. She'd liked the older woman almost immediately despite their limited interaction. Kate ran her diner with a brisk efficiency and, though she came across as gruff sometimes, she had a bit of a soft side. Regis had seen the woman give a harsh word to a man who'd been unreasonably impatient with one of her servers during the rush hour, and then slip an extra cookie to a little boy who'd just been told that his dog had died.

Kate set a pie on the counter and took off the mitts. "And you'll have to ignore my son. Hawk seems to think I'd lose my head if it weren't attached."

"Mom," Keith countered. "Did you or did you not put a spoon in your pocket at work and forget about it until you found it in the washer?"

Kate made a dismissive noise. "When you've got as much on your mind as I do, that's normal."

"And your excuse for spending twenty minutes looking for your glasses when you were wearing them?"

Regis couldn't help but enjoy the playful bickering as Kate and Keith wiped down the counter together, one on each side.

"Excuse me," Regis said, not really wanting to interrupt. But she felt bad just standing there while they worked. "How can I help?"

"You can have a seat," Kate answered. "You're a guest."

"Please," Regis pressed. "I can't just let you do all the work."

"Very well," Kate said, ignoring Keith's exasperated sigh. "I'll take out the last of the food and you can wash the dishes while Hawk puts them away." She paused, giving Keith a meaningful look. "I'll get everyone on their way. We should all be out of your hair soon. By the way, honey, I put some leftovers in containers in your fridge. They should be good for a few days."

"That's an awfully big smile on your face, Ma," Keith said.

Kate's smile got bigger. "Yes, it is. Sam is coming home."

Keith's face brightened. "You're going to have all your boys in one place at the same time."

Kate's smile faltered just a little. "Well, not all. Only God's going to provide that. But I'll take my four boys together here in Rudolph for as long as I can have them."

"How long is he staying this time?"

"At least the whole summer. He'll be working to clear some of the damaged areas down here because the threat of fire will be higher this summer after all this flooding left debris everywhere." Kate was almost giddy with excitement as she talked.

"Ah, so that's the reason for the smile," Keith said. He hugged his mom and then turned to face Regis as he spoke. "My brother Sam works with a Hotshot fire crew out of Colorado. But he's like you. He goes where the action is."

"And this summer, I aim to enjoy having you all home." Kate turned to Regis. "Thanks for the help, dear. Enjoy your evening."

Kate picked up the pie from the counter and headed out into the other room. A few seconds later, Regis heard the door shut and then quiet. After all that commotion, she was finally alone with Keith.

Regis walked over to the sink and turned on the faucet, feeling the water with her hand until it got to a hot enough temperature to wash dishes. "Your mom's great," she said as Keith came up alongside her.

"Yeah, she is." The three words were full of love and again, that feeling of envy filled her. After a moment, Keith continued. "You know, you really don't have to wash dishes.

You've had as long a day as everyone else, and I promised you dinner."

"This is fine," Regis assured him as she began to wash a mixing bowl.

She was thankful that her back was to Keith so she didn't have to see his weak in the knees kind of smile. But to top all that, he had a wonderful mother whom he clearly adored, and was committed to doing charity work in his community. If she'd been unable to get him out of her mind before, today had just made it ten times worse. She shoved the thought aside and forced herself to concentrate on the slippery bowl in her hand.

"Leave these," Keith said, pulling her from her thoughts and making her jump. He was a lot closer than she'd realized. She could smell the crisp scent of him, all male and one hundred percent appealing. "You came over so I could feed you, not so you could wash dishes."

"It's fine," Regis smiled. "It's nice to be doing something so simple. Gets my mind off of things."

"You'll have to tell me about those 'things' later. But to be honest, I'm starved, so we might as well start those pizzas or we're never going to eat."

"I have a better idea," she said, turning the faucet off.

"What's that?"

"Leftovers. Your mom just said she left you some leftovers in the refrigerator. They're probably still warm, and if they're not, we can just heat them up quickly."

"That's cheating." His answer brought a bubble of laughter from her. "My mom made that, not me. This was supposed to be something special."

"Look, I'm starved, too. I don't know if I can wait for pizza when I know your mom's home cooking is on the other side of that door. And you and I both know her cooking is good. We can do pizza another night."

"Another night, huh? Thinking ahead. I like that."

"Well, let's get through this one first."

Keith pulled her into his arms and gave her a warm hug that made her head spin. When he released her, he said, "You're a woman after my own heart. I'll get a fire going in the living room if you want to heat up some of that food."

"That sounds like a plan."

Keith pulled two dishes out of the cabinet and put them on the counter. Regis waved him away with her hands.

"I can find everything we need. Go make that fire."

Twenty minutes later, they were sitting cross-legged on a blanket in front of the floor to ceiling stone fireplace eating the dinner Kate had made. There was a corked bottle of wine resting against the sofa next to Keith and a half-full glass of wine that Regis was drinking with dinner. If not for the food she was eating, the wine would surely be going to her head and making her sleepy.

"I don't know how your mom manages to feed so many people like this."

"She doesn't do it alone. There are a whole lot of people who are working round the clock trying to set everything to right around here."

"Like you."

Hawk shrugged, embarrassed. "After the flood, there were so many families that lost so much. The need grew, so I just helped fill in like everyone else. It's the least we can do."

"How bad was it?" Regis asked.

"I watched the water coming down off of the higher points." Hawk looked down at his hands, lost in a memory that must seem so vivid to him. This was his home. It wasn't just some other place that he saw on the news. "This part of town is high enough that I wasn't in any real danger, but Logan's place is on lower ground, and he was there alone with Keith when the flood waters came in fast and furious. It covered most of his pastures. He'd moved his animals so his damage was minimal. But it managed to get all the way up to the barn, which was close enough.

"When the rain stopped, I went out with a lot of others to try to help rescue people who were stuck. It's weird the images that stick with you during something like this. I saw the Hardwicks rowing a canoe across their field. The Joyners' boy was in a tree for almost two hours before rescuers could get to him." Hawk took a deep breath and tossed his paper napkin into the fire. "I think over the following week, I set a dozen broken bones, sewed up hundreds of cuts and gave tetanus shots to half the town."

"This is one of the worst disaster areas I've seen," Reggie said. "Definitely the worst flood. Thank you again for helping me the other day. I'm not sure I could have gotten through all the properties I did without your help."

Regis looked up from her plate and her stomach clenched. Keith was finished eating and was leaning against the sofa with a beer in his hand. The heat in his eyes was unmistakable. It had been a long time since a man had looked at her like that.

"What are you looking at?"

His smile widened. "You. I like looking at you."

She put down her fork. "I can see that. What I can't understand is why?"

"You have a little hook nose. Did you know that? And there is one little cluster of freckles that are bunched up high on one of your cheeks."

Her hand immediately went to the place he spoke of. Usually she spent time to cover up that spot. It had plagued her when she was a teenager. But she was so busy these days she hardly noticed it.

Keith leaned over and pulled her hand away. "I like it."

She giggled. "And you're strange, Keith McKinnon."

"And I like very much the way you say my name."

SHE WAS BLUSHING AGAIN. It amazed Hawk how easily he could get Regis to blush about the simplest things. The woman loved to put up a tough front, but inside she was as smooth as silk. She had a big heart, and he wanted so much to know that heart in every way.

"Why doesn't anyone but your nephew call you Keith? Even your mother called you Hawk."

"There's no real mystery really."

"Then tell me the story. Why does everyone call you Hawk?"

"It goes way back," he said. "I was on a scouts' camping trip with my brother, Wade. I must have been six or seven at the time. My dad was one of the scout leaders back then. Anyway, we'd gone on what seemed like a long hike down in the Black Hills. When we got back up to base camp, the other scout leader noticed he wasn't wearing his wedding ring. Anyway, we all looked around the ground at camp for about an hour, and no one could find it. But I'd remembered seeing something when we were hiking, so I decided to investigate."

"You all went back out on the trail after being there all day?"

"No. Just me."

"At six or seven? On your own?"

"Seemed like a good plan at the time. Anyway, I hiked down the trail and went back to the place where I'd seen the sun was hitting this shiny thing below, and sure enough, it was a wedding ring. I felt like I'd struck a vein of gold. I didn't realize they'd sent a search team out to find me. And when we all got back to base camp, my father was ripping mad. But I told my story about how I'd seen the ring up from high on the trail. Then I proudly pulled the ring out of my pocket and gave it to the scout leader."

"Aw, he must have been so happy to get his ring back."

Hawk couldn't help but laugh. "It wasn't his."

"What?"

"It was someone else's wedding ring. We found out when we got home that the other scout leader found his ring at home on his nightstand."

"He'd never even lost his ring?"

Keith shook his head as he thought of how Wade tried to defend him. "Wade used to tell the story about how I had eyes like a hawk to find that little wedding ring from high up on the trail, and if anyone was missing anything, they should come to me first because I'd find it. The nickname stuck with my friends and eventually with my family. I think my mom just gave up calling me Keith because it was easier to get me to answer to Hawk. Not even my teachers called me Keith. It was usually, 'Mr. McKinnon' in response to something I was getting in trouble for. I'm surprised I ever made it out of high school. Even my patients call me Hawk since most of them have known me my entire life. And if they haven't, they call me Doc."

"And with your nephew?"

His chest filled with pride. "Well, that's special between the two of us."

She shifted in place and shrugged. "I didn't realize I was treading on sacred ground."

"But I like the way *you* say my name," he said. "Your eyes sparkle when you say it."

Her mouth dropped open. "They do not."

"And your voice changes." A tiny voice in the back of Hawk's mind wondered what it would be like to hear Regis say his name when they were making love. And the two of them making love was something he'd thought a whole lot about ever since he'd kissed Regis the other night at the mill.

She was looking at him intently, and he wondered if his thoughts were giving him away. And yet, she didn't look away or blush. She just studied his face and then ... there it was in her eyes. The sparkle.

"Come here," he said, moving closer to her until he could feel the heat of her body more than the heat of the fire. "I like having you close by."

"Oh, really?" she teased with a smile.

"I like you. A lot."

She drew in a deep breath and looked into his eyes. He reached up and touched her hair, pushing a few silky strands away from her forehead. He let his hands trail down the side of her cheek until he found that adorable cluster of freckles that had consumed his thoughts for days. He brushed his thumb over it and then bent his head to place a soft kiss on her cheek. But before he could do it, Regis lifted her face to him with her mouth slightly parted.

"Not yet," he said, when it was clear her mouth was seeking his. "I want to look at you. Discover you. Know all of you."

The flame of fire that lit her eyes sent sparks flying through him, settling deep in his chest and lighting a fire below his belly. He wanted her more than he wanted his next breath and couldn't think of anything else.

As Hawk moved to give her what she wanted, what he wanted, Regis shifted closer to him and then winced. He pulled back quickly. "Did I hurt you?"

She reached up and wrapped her arm around his shoulder as if she didn't want him to move too far away. "I just pressed my leg against the ground. Forget it." Then she lifted her face to him as she did earlier, wanting him as much as he wanted her. His mouth claimed her instantly, playing, teasing, tasting and then devouring until he thought he'd lost his mind.

As he wrapped one arm around her waist and placed his hand at the nape of her neck, Regis's hand made a slow journey from his stomach and up his chest until she abruptly stopped.

Pulling back, he saw her confused expression as she touched his chest. Not wanting the distraction, he reached inside his shirt and pulled out the chain and medallion he always wore.

"Is it going to bother you?"

She shook her head and touched the cross and medallion with her fingers. "I just wondered what it was."

Relieved Hawk went back to the very thing that was driving him crazy. As he kissed her cheek, he breathed in the sweet scent of her and made a trail of kisses along her face until he nestled his face against her neck and kissed her there. He heard her soft moan of pleasure and it only surged him on.

"Keith?"

With a ragged breath, he dragged himself from the source of his pleasure to look at her. He couldn't remember the last time he was out of his mind wanting a woman, and now, he realized he'd never wanted a woman more than he wanted Regis right now.

SHE WAS COMING COMPLETELY unglued by Keith's every touch. Regis couldn't think. She couldn't breathe. She dug her fingers into his shoulders, and for a second, she questioned whether she should even be considering getting involved with Keith McKinnon, much less making love with him. And she hoped with every fiber of her being that this was leading to that because she couldn't think of anything other than getting gloriously naked with this man.

As he gazed at her with the same desire that was like a drug to her, his eyes were questioning. There were no more questions in her mind. With her fingers, she pulled at the buttons of her shirt. He watched her attentively as each button slipped out of place until her shirt was fully free, and she pushed it aside. He freed her the rest of the way by slipping it off her shoulders and dropping it to the floor. She undid the front clasp of her bra under his watchful eye and marveled at the blaze of fire that ignited in his eyes as her breasts fell free of their restraints.

"I don't know how much more of this I can handle," he said, slipping out of his shirt and tossing it somewhere else in the room. Regis giggled as they rid themselves of the rest of their clothes, pushing them aside so they had the full spread of the blanket Keith had laid out in front of the fire for them to lay on.

And when they lay next to each other, hot flesh against hot flesh, Regis thought she'd lose her mind again. His hands were everywhere, stroking her skin, touching her in places that made her throw back her head in pure pleasure. And then he explored her more, this time with his mouth. He kissed her, leaving a moist trail down her neck, to her breasts as he stroked one breast with his wide palm and then drove her crazy by flicking her nipple with his tongue.

"Oh, I want you inside me," she said, not sure where she'd had the strength to even utter the words aloud. She reached between them, stroked him and wrapped her leg around him. He threw his head back with a gasp, breathing heavy, and then with determination, he kissed her with such passion and fire that she lost all sense of where she was. All she knew was their two bodies entwined, touching each other, loving each other.

And when he entered her with such force and hunger, all it took was a few strokes to lift her higher until she reached her peak and tumbled over the edge. She was still feeling the incredible pleasure he'd brought her when he rocked his hip harder. He buried his face in her neck and breathed harder until he reached his orgasm with an intensity that had him gasping for breath and clinging to her.

In his arms, Regis closed her eyes and wrapped her arms and legs around Keith, not wanting to let go of the beautiful connection they'd created. And as he pulled away from her and gazed into her eyes with such longing, she wondered if it was possible to ever get her fill of Keith McKinnon.

Chapter Seven

THE FIRE WAS WARM AGAINST her naked skin. Keith's body nestled up against hers made it all the warmer. He'd pulled a small blanket that had been draped over the chair by the fireplace and loosely placed it over them. Content, she watched the changing colors of the fire licking the burning logs as she rested her head on Keith's shoulder. With his arm wrapped around, he held her close.

She played with the gold medallion and cross he was wearing.

"Where did you get these?"

He glanced down and took the medallion between his fingers. "This was Wade's. Remember that ring I found in the canyon?"

"Yeah."

"Wade melted it down and made it into this. If you noticed, there are only markings on one side of the medallion. He always wore it, too."

"How did you get it?"

Keith drew in a deep breath, expanding his chest. She felt the rise and fall of it and the heavy thump of his heartbeat against her ear as she lay there.

"Wade was leaving for the Peace Corps. He'd been gone for a while and was back for a visit before heading out again. As you can imagine, my mother wasn't too pleased."

"She likes having her boys around."

"Could you tell?"

Regis chuckled.

"Anyway, Wade called all of us who were still stateside and wanted to meet for a drink before he left. Ethan was overseas in the military. Sam was in Arizona, I think, fighting some monster fire that had broken out there. Logan, well, he was dealing with his life back then, which was ...difficult."

"And you?"

"I was doing my residency in Sioux City. Wade was in Aberdeen, just a few hours from Sioux City."

Keith was quiet and just rolled the medallion between his fingers.

"Logan went to have a drink with Wade, and I didn't. Next time I saw Logan, he gave me the chain with the medallion and this cross and told me Wade wanted me to hold onto it until he came back. I put it around my neck, and the next day we found out about the tsunami that hit the island he was working on. They never found him."

She gasped and lifted her head to look at Keith. The unshed tears in his eyes were illuminated by the dying fire.

"I've never taken this off since," he said, looking directly at her. "I've never told anyone else that story."

She sat up and touched his chest in an effort to comfort him. She didn't care that she was naked and her breasts were fully exposed in probably the most unflattering position.

"What about the cross?" she asked.

"That's the odd thing. I don't know anything about this cross. I knew so much about my brother. Of all my brothers, I was closest to Wade. But I don't know how he got it or why he wore it. He used to only have the medallion on the chain. But this is the way Wade gave it to Logan, so I kept it that way. It makes me feel like ... he's close by somehow."

She lay back down against Keith, and he pulled her close to him.

"Like a part of him is always with you," she added.

Keith lifted his head a fraction and looked down at her, but said nothing. Then he lay back again.

"I have my mother's hairbrush," she finally said. "It's nothing special. It's just a big silver brush. I don't even know if it's real silver or just plated. She couldn't take living on bases and moving all around the world."

"With your dad gone so much, I'm surprised she didn't take you with her."

"Yeah, well, she didn't like family life so much either, and having a six-year-old in tow didn't fit into the next phase of her life."

He cursed quietly and shook his head. "Sorry," he said.

"Why? Because of my mother or your foul mouth?" she said chuckling. "Remember, I lived on Army bases. You couldn't possibly say something I haven't already heard."

Keith chuckled too and then became quiet again.

"It doesn't really matter though. It's just a hairbrush," she said. "I just ... with all the moving, I was never able to let it go."

He squeezed her harder until she thought they couldn't get closer. And still she wanted more. She wanted to feel that connection she'd felt when they'd made love.

She lifted up on her side and put her arm around him. "Keith?"

"Hmm?" he said, his voice groggy.

"The fire is dying."

"Do you want another blanket?"

She smiled and kissed him slowly. "I had something else in mind."

She felt his smile against her lips and felt the thundering of his heartbeat beneath her palm. Then he said, "I like the way you think."

THE NEXT FEW WEEKS had been the happiest Regis had ever known. She spent the mornings working in the senior center with a long line of people filing in to ask questions and fill out paperwork. Some afternoons she'd go on the road with Keith and visit properties. She'd listen to the stories about the people she'd meet and at night, the two of them would lock themselves in his log home and make love.

Soon the number of people needing help grew shorter, and somewhere in the back of Regis's mind, she knew her time in Rudolph was close to coming to an end. But she'd decided to relish each and every moment she had with Keith for as long as she possibly could.

And then came the afternoon when she knew all that love and beauty was in jeopardy. She answered her cell phone call from her manager as she stepped into the motel room, wondering why she even bothered to keep it since she'd been spending every night for the past two weeks with Keith.

"Is there a problem?" she asked Mike.

He hesitated a fraction. "You're doing great there. I'm just wondering why you've sent this claim for the Buxton Mills through with a recommendation for full replacement when it's clear it was flood damage."

She dropped her briefcase on the bed and sat down next to it. "The roof and siding show that the ice storm did some damage to the property. I have pictures to support that."

"I see them, and I don't dispute that. But I also see the water line on the inside of the property showing that there was a flood."

She bit her bottom lip. "There was. The property is on the river. But the ice and rain did the damage to the structure."

Mike's heavy sigh sounded distorted through the phone. "You're one of the most thorough adjusters I have, Regis. But this one is cut and dry. They have flood insurance, so the most we can approve for this is what is listed in their policy. We can repair the roof although I have my doubts it was the storm that damaged that and the siding. My records show this property has been empty for quite some time."

"The amount of the payout for those won't be enough to cover the structural damage."

"You need a vacation, Regis. You're getting attached again. I'm sorry, but I can't approve the full amount of this claim. If you'd prefer it, I'll send the letter."

She closed her eyes to the disappointment filling her. "No, I'll do it."

"Fine. Regis?"

"Yes?"

"Why don't you pack up. I'm sure you're tired and could use a break. I'm not kidding about the vacation."

"I'm not done here."

"End of the week you are. I'll bring in someone else to give you a break."

"But—" she started to argue, but he'd already hung up.

She was leaving. But before she could do that, she had to break the bad news to some people who'd counted on her.

"ARE YOU ALL RIGHT?" Keith's voice brought Regis out of her reverie as she sat at the kitchen table and cradled her morning coffee in her hand. She tried not to read too much into the concern in his voice. Things were complicated enough as it was. She decided it was probably a good idea to keep things simple. There was no reason to bring up the reasons for her insomnia.

"I didn't sleep well last night."

"I noticed."

"I'm sorry. Did I keep you awake?"

"No, but clearly something kept you awake. What was it?"

She shrugged. She hadn't written up the letter to the town yet about the outcome of the claim for the Buxton Mill. She wanted to write it and then tell Ian McKinnon personally. He'd worked hard on plans to develop the property for the town that he deserved to hear it from her first.

"You're awfully quiet," Keith finally broke the silence, bringing his empty coffee cup to the sink. "Something is bothering you."

Regis glanced over at Keith's handsome face. When had she become this attached to seeing it, having it bring her comfort.

"I have a lot of work to do before I leave."

His expression fell. "You're leaving?"

"End of the week. I got the call from my supervisor yesterday."

He opened his mouth to say something, but then stopped.

"I knew last night," she said, answering the question he didn't put into words. "I just didn't know ... how to tell you. I didn't want to talk about it." She abruptly got up from the table, dumped the rest of her coffee in the sink and turned on the faucet to rinse the sink and her cup.

"Stop," Keith said.

She didn't look at him. "I don't want to leave these dishes in the sink."

"Stop," he said again, turning off the water and pulling her around to face him.

"We knew this day was going to come eventually," she said, looking up at him. The light in his blue eyes had faded with his disappointment.

"Did we?

A cynical laugh escaped her lips. "How could you not know that I'd be leaving?"

"I don't know. I didn't really think much about it. I just thought about how I was feeling. How I thought we were both feeling."

She fought tears as he pulled her into his arms. "Right now, I'm feeling rotten. To make matters worse, my boss is insisting on my taking a vacation."

With raised eyebrows, Keith said, "Well, there's an excuse for you to stay longer."

She pulled out of his arms and went back to the sink. "I can't even think that far. There is still so much for me to do this week."

"Okay, here's a radical idea."

She stopped washing a coffee cup and glanced at him.

"Stay."

"What?"

"Finish out your week and then just stay. You said you have vacation. So take a vacation right here. You don't have to run off to another town, do you?"

"Well, no."

"Where do you go when you leave a town you've been working in?"

"I have a simple apartment in Chicago. By simple, I mean utilitarian. It looks a lot like my motel room except it has a small kitchen. I'm not there very often. I'm sure once I get home Mike will find another town for me to go to. He usually keeps me busy."

Keith leaned against the counter as she finished rinsing the last dish and put it in the strainer to dry. She turned off the water and dried her hands before looking at Keith again.

When she did, she saw emotion in his eyes that she'd never seen. Not even when they'd made love. A lump of emotion formed in her throat that she couldn't swallow down.

"Stay," he said in a soft voice that was almost pleading. Her bottom lip began to quiver, and she clamped it down with her teeth to keep it steady.

"This isn't something we should talk about this morning."

He looked at her for a lingering moment as if studying the lines on her face.

"Okay, we'll talk about it tonight then."

She nodded and reached up to kiss him. He tasted of coffee and smelled like the cinnamon bagels they'd had for breakfast. His tongue brushed against her lips, and she gasped. The hand at the small of her back flexed, pressing her closer to him as he tilted his head, deepening the kiss until she was lost in him again.

Everything that had been circling in her head since last night vanished. All she thought about was the way it felt when this incredible man kissed her. He'd turned her world inside out. And yet all that disappeared when she was in Keith's arms. There was absolutely no confusion about the way his mouth felt against hers, the way his lips moved, how his tongue teased at the seam of her mouth. She had no doubts about whether or not she wanted him to keep kissing her, about how right it felt to have him holding her.

When they finally broke apart, their breath was coming in pants, and she could feel Keith's heart beating as furiously as her own. He kept his arms around her and looked down at her.

"I'll see you tonight," he said with a smile.

And for the first time in the past two weeks, Regis dreaded it.

Chapter Eight

"THIS IS THE SECOND time I've caught you daydreaming," Nancy said, standing in the doorway to Hawk's office.

"I'm not daydreaming," he said.

"Yeah? Well, whatever it is, if you don't snap out of it, I'll be forced to do something drastic."

"Like what?"

"Call your mother." She chuckled at the look he gave her, and then tapped her fingers on the doorjamb. "Seriously, you've got a patient in examining room one who is waiting for you."

"I'll be right there."

Ever since Regis left his house yesterday morning, he knew she was pulling away from him. She told him she was going to be finished with her work in Rudolph by the end of the week. But Hawk didn't think she'd avoid him before she had to leave. But then, just as he was expecting her to come to his house last night after work, she'd called and said she had too much paperwork, and thought it was better for her to stay at the motel.

He'd spent many nights alone in that big log cabin since he'd come back to Rudolph after med school. But last night was the first night in over two weeks that he'd spent the night without Regis snuggled up, warm, and naked next to him. And he didn't like it one bit.

He got up from behind his desk and walked the few strides to the examining room, pulling the folder from the wall file and checking the contents. Concerned, he knocked on the door and went inside.

Ian McKinnon sat in a chair by the window instead of the examining table. And he didn't look happy, which was great concern to Hawk.

"I didn't expect to see you here today."

"I didn't plan on coming." He turned his hand. That's when Hawk saw the white rag stained with red. "I slammed the glass on the counter and cut myself."

"On purpose?"

"The slamming of the glass was on purpose. The glass breaking was just Murphy's Law."

Hawk washed his hands and dried them quickly before putting on latex gloves. Ian sat in the same chair by the window. Hawk sat in his seat and rolled it closer to his cousin to examine the wound.

"You may need a stitch or two," he said.

"Terrific," Ian said.

"What set this off?"

"The phone call I got last night from your girlfriend."

Hawk stopped examining the wound and looked at Ian. Dark circles were evident under his eyes.

"Regis called you? What for?"

"The claim for the mill wasn't fully approved. What they're giving us is a joke. We can forget getting the mill rehabbed for the center. There isn't enough money to fix what needs to be repaired. The engineer said the flood water caused structural damage to the foundation of the building and needs to be completely repaired or the building will have to be torn down. Except, the insurance company is only giving us cleanup cost for the building."

"What about FEMA aid?"

"What? In two years? The repairs need to be made within a certain period of time. Without enough money to repair the foundation the floods destroyed, the town will order the building to be completely torn down. That means no more Wounded Veterans Center. "

Now it all made sense to him. "I'll talk to her."

"She can't do anything. At least, that's what she said. It came from higher up. Oh, and she's really sorry."

Hawk squashed down his anger as best he could. Why hadn't Regis come and told him about the claim for the mill herself? Why was he getting it second-hand?

"Let's put that aside for now and get you stitched up."

"What's the hurry? It's not like I have anything pressing to do with my day now that the project at the mill is all but dead."

Ian might be ready to give up. But Hawk was a long way from giving up the fight.

THE COMMUNITY CENTER was busier than it had been in days now that a full FEMA staff had set up camp there. People were coming in and out of the room from morning until late afternoon. Regis was glad she'd gotten most of the paperwork for her claims finished. Now she was just fielding questions and dealing with disgruntled customers who weren't happy.

She was tired, physically from lack of sleep, and emotionally from dealing with a heart so heavy, it physically hurt. She'd hated sleeping alone last night. Regis hated even more that each time she rolled over, she'd searched for Keith's warm body. Not finding him there left her cold.

She forced herself to be in the present and not the past. She had too much work to do to spend time pining over a man who'd be part of her past very soon.

The main area of the community room was full of people. Some were filling out paperwork, others were lined up in front of a table. Off to one side, a group of older kids watched their younger siblings playing while harried parents waited for their turn in line with the FEMA reps. Luckily, no one was lining up in front of her table needing help. It gave her some time to go through paperwork that needed to be finalized and filed by the end of the week before she left.

She heard a familiar voice greet someone in the crowd and lifted her gaze from the computer screen long enough to see Keith charging her way. The look on his face made her stomach drop.

"Can I talk to you a minute in private?" He didn't bother with preliminaries as he stepped behind the table.

Regis looked up, startled. She braced herself for what she knew was coming.

"Can it wait until later? I really want to finish this paperwork before the end of the day. Maybe we could have dinner out somewhere tonight," she said.

"This is important," Hawk insisted. "There is an empty room down the hall. We can talk there."

"All right." She quickly asked the agent at the next table to watch her computer while she stepped away, a courtesy they did for each other during the day when it got busy and promised to be quick.

She followed Keith to an empty room down the hall and waited for him to shut the door behind her. She didn't wait for him to get to what was on his mind.

"I didn't tell you because I thought Ian should know first."

"That was very thoughtful of you. But that doesn't change the fact that the Buxton Mill claim has been denied."

"It wasn't denied. It just wasn't approved for the full amount."

"It may as well have been denied for all the good that tiny settlement will do for the cause."

"Keith," Regis shifted, uncomfortable with his question. "You know that I'm not really supposed to discuss my cases."

"Ian isn't a case," he spat out the word. "You should have seen him, Regis. He's given up. That center was a lifeline for him and now ..."

She closed her eyes and tried to steady her nerves. This had been her fear.

"I did everything I could do, Keith. These things aren't always as cut and dry as you think. Every claim has certain criteria that need to be met if it's going to be approved. I skated on thin ice with my report, but I got called on it by my manager. The pictures clearly show flood damage inside the building. That water level was enough to show that it was flood water, not the rain, wind or ice that damaged the property. I can only pay out for how the policy reads. Believe me, I wish the damage had been done by wind and ice. It would have been easier to approve more for the claim."

"The engineer said the foundation needs to completely be replaced or the building needs to be demolished. If you read the report."

"I had the engineer's report. Ian gave it to me. But, unfortunately, the engineer also said that the foundation showed signs of wear before the storms. The building was aging. The insurance company won't pay out for an aging property that was already in disrepair."

"So that's it?"

"There's nothing else I can do."

Keith paced in front of her, clearly upset by what his cousin was going through. Then he stopped and looked at her directly.

"Is that why you didn't stay with me last night?"

She drew in a slow breath. "I needed to call Ian and prepare the letter to the town. I wanted to make sure it was thorough."

"That's an excuse. You could have done that at my place."

"You know I wouldn't have worked if I had stayed at your house last night." She smiled up at him and was taken aback when he didn't respond in kind.

"If we can't get the money to repair Buxton Mill, it'll have to be demolished. The town won't let it stand in that condition while we raise money."

She'd never felt so helpless in her life or wanted to do something more than what she could do for anyone. "I know. And I'm sorry."

"Are you?"

His accusation was like a slap to the face. "What the hell is that supposed to mean?"

"You blow into town, take a quick look at a policy or a property and decide the fate of people's lives. And then you get the hell out of town again and leave the people left behind to pick up the pieces."

Anger surged in her. "Yes, that's what I do. That's all I do. But in doing that I'm trying to help people just like you do, Keith. It may not be the same, but I can help some people. There are times when I can't. Sometimes my hands are tied."

He paced in front of her again. "Ethan served eight years in the Navy, Regis. Ian did two tours in Iraq, lost his leg and nearly lost his life. This center was important to the soldiers in this community coming home from service overseas. It was supposed to be a place where they could come together and deal with whatever they experienced while serving this country. They need this center."

"Do you think I don't know that? Believe me, I have been around active military and veterans my entire life. But it doesn't change what I can and can't do for the center."

Keith ran his hand over his head in frustration. "Jeez, Logan and Poppy were talking about getting married there. Now that's not going to happen either."

She took in the heavy slump of Keith's shoulders and felt it herself. She was losing this battle. And maybe it was never a battle that could be won. This is what she'd always dreaded, falling for someone and then having to disappoint them.

Keith pierced her with a pleading look. "They'll never get the building inspector to approve repairs without the money. And without the money the mill will have to be demolished and that'll be the end of the community center for the veterans. They need help."

"I know." She glanced at the door and thought about all the people waiting in line. Every one of them was feeling as desperate as Keith felt.

"I can't help everyone. But I can help some of the people in there," she said, pointing out the door. "I need to get back to doing that."

Keith nodded. "You're right. Okay."

"I'll understand if you don't want me to come over tonight."

"No, I do."

With a wary smile, she said. "I'll see you then."

HAWK WATCHED REGIS walk down the hallway until she disappeared in the room that was mulling with activity. Every emotion inside him was raw and conflicted, making it hard for him to even think. Deep down he knew this wasn't Regis's fault. She didn't make the rules, and there were a whole lot of rules that were stacked against them.

But part of his frustration went deeper than the center. She hadn't told him what was going on. Instead, she'd avoided him last night. She was leaving. She'd said as much the other day at breakfast. And that was the harder pill for him to swallow than losing out on insurance claim money for the mill. It was losing Regis that was eating him up inside.

If he was going to fight, then the fight started there.

Chapter Nine

REGIS SAT IN HER CAR in front of Keith's house for a minute, hoping that tonight would turn out better than this afternoon had. She'd reminded herself a thousand times over the course of the afternoon why she didn't get involved. It was for this. There was always going to be someone leaving. And leaving was just as hard when you cared about someone as being left behind.

But she wouldn't deny herself the chance to spend as much time as she could with Keith before she left Rudolph. She hoped he felt the same.

She checked her hair and make-up again in her rearview mirror and tried to push away the memory of her confrontation with Keith earlier. She'd known he would be upset about the Buxton Mill claim. But she had no idea how deep his feelings for it went. She only hoped they could get past that tonight.

The moment she entered the house, it was clear that her hopes had been in vain. A meal was set out on the table, and the lights were low, but the normal easiness of their nights together was gone. Instead, Keith sat at one end of the table and ate his dinner while she silently ate hers.

Regis looked down at her plate, trying to figure out what she could say that would fix this. She picked at her food, pushing it around on her plate with her fork, unable to eat any of it. Her stomach was in knots, waiting for Keith to say something, anything that would indicate what he was thinking. But she already knew. She'd been through many nights like this right before her father would ship out on a tour.

"Maybe this wasn't such a good idea," she finally said.

Keith looked at her then, questions clouding his handsome face. "What? You coming here or us?"

"Both."

"You can't mean that."

She didn't. She couldn't imagine not having spent these last few weeks with Keith, and yet, part of her wished she hadn't. It would be so much easier to leave.

"I'm leaving in two days, Keith. It's not going to get any easier."

"Then stay," Keith said. There was more there, in his eyes and in his voice. But he said no more.

She shook her head slowly. "I'm no good in one place."

"That's an excuse not to face what you feel."

"Really?"

Frustration shadowed his normal happy-go-lucky expression. He got up from the table and dropped his plate into the sink, the sound of it jarring her.

"You've spent a lifetime leaving people behind, Regis. Aren't you tired yet?"

"Correction. People left me behind."

"And you followed suit."

She started to protest, to argue the same clichéd points she'd convinced herself of all these years. But those arguments were bogus. They just fell flat in her mind, and she knew she'd lose as soon as the words came out of her mouth.

She did leave. Just like her mother had. Just like everyone else who'd left her behind. It was easier that way.

"Stay," he said again. This time, his eyes were pleading. "Stay long enough to see if something is real. To see if there's anything here worth holding on to."

Her bottom lip threatened to betray her with a slight quiver. "That's easy for you to say. To imagine. You have this fantastic family and wonderful friends you've known since the cradle. Everyone in this town has memories that go all the way back to the dinosaurs." She laughed at the absurdity of her statement, but at its core, Regis had meant it.

Hope filled his eyes. "You could have that, too."

She shook her head quickly. "How? All I have are faces. I don't even remember the names anymore. They're all blurred into one."

"Then stay and let someone love you. Let someone leave an imprint on your heart. I want so much to do that. You have no idea."

"You say that because you've never had anyone you loved leave you before. I have."

"That's where you're wrong. My best friend left me, and he's never coming back."

Her heart stopped just seeing the anguish on Keith's face.

"Do you know what the last thing was that I said to Wade? 'I can't.' Those are two words I regret more than anything."

"You couldn't know what was going to happen."

He nodded. "No, but it doesn't change what did. All he wanted to do was have a few beers with his brothers before he left for his tour with the Peace Corps. I was in the middle of my residency in Sioux City, working eighty hours a week. I didn't want to lose precious sleep to drive the few hours to meet him halfway between Sioux City and Aberdeen and then drive back.

"Regis, I think about that phone call with Wade all the time. I would change that in a heartbeat if I could. I missed my opportunity to say good-bye to my brother. Of course, I never would have known at the time it was my last chance. But if I'd known, I would have driven all night and worked all day to have that last laugh or last hug from him before he boarded that plane."

"I understand your loss. But there's a difference. Wade didn't leave you on purpose. My mother did. She just ... left."

"This isn't about loss, Regis. It's about risk. I was so focused on becoming a doctor and doing well at my residency that I didn't risk stepping out of my comfort zone to do something that was probably one of the most important moments of my life; my opportunity to see my brother one last time. I would have been fine. I'd pulled all-nighters before, working two days straight without sleep."

"This isn't the same thing."

"Then why are you leaving? Why not stay and take a risk? You and I both know there's something special here. I've never felt the way I feel about you before. No other woman in my life has even come close. Even though you're too stubborn to admit it, I have a feeling you feel the same. Except the closer we get, the more you want to run. That's the real reason why you didn't want to stay last night."

Tears filled her eyes. "I'm no good in one place."

"How do you know that? You don't even let yourself get close to finding out."

She sighed. "I just know."

"What are you so afraid of? Needing someone?"

"I don't need anyone," she said. It was a standard line and one she let herself believe for a long time. And she knew this time she was lying to herself.

"Then you're in better shape than me because I need you."

She shook her head. "How is that possible?"

"It's true. I've spent my entire adult life pushing forward with tunnel vision. But one thing became crystal clear to me yesterday when I woke up and you weren't next to me. I need you, Regis. And I thought, 'What if she doesn't come back. Ever.' I couldn't handle that. And suddenly I didn't know how I was going to get through the day."

"This can't end good, Keith. I'm leaving in two days."

"Then don't leave. Stay with me, Regis. Stay and find out if what we have is more than just a passing fling."

She jolted back at his words. "Fling? Do you really think that's what this has been for me?"

"How would I know anything? You're pulling away again. You've got so much armor guarding your heart that I can't get in to see it. Where is your heart, Regis? I want to love you. Let me love you."

The tears she'd been holding back were falling now. "You're not the only one who lost someone, Keith."

"I know your mother hurt you."

"I'm not talking about my mother. Or my father's endless tours and being left behind." She sighed. "I can't even believe I'm telling you this."

"Tell me," he said, pulling her closer. But she needed her distance and turned toward the table, sitting down before he spoke.

"I told you I've lived on bases all over the world. Well, as you can imagine, there weren't a whole lot of eligible guys to date other than young military men. I'd met someone when I was eighteen. His name was David, and he was a year older than me. My father was gone, and I was staying with a family on base when we met. I'd been getting ready to leave for college, but I stayed because of David. I thought I was in love with him. I'd had crushes on servicemen before, but this was different. He was my first kiss, my first love, my first everything."

She shrugged, sure that Keith understood her meaning. When he didn't say anything, she went on.

"David was sent to Iraq early on. We wrote. Talked to each other whenever we could. And then I didn't hear from him for a while. Everyone told me not to worry because he was probably in some remote place, and the mail would catch up eventually. It did. I got a letter from his sister in the States telling me he'd been killed."

Empathy showed on Keith's face, making her want to weep. "You loved him," he said.

She nodded. She hadn't known at the time, but she'd realized too late just how much she had loved David.

"You see, I've spent a lifetime of seeing people go, living with families who were suffering through waiting for people to come home, and sometimes they never did. You ask me where my heart is? It broke a long time ago. How many times can a heart break before it never heals, Keith? And you want me to risk it again?"

She couldn't hold back the tears. "This was a bad idea." She went into the living room, grabbed her coat and purse and headed for the door.

"Where are you going?"

"Back to the motel."

"You don't have to do that."

But she was already out the door.

THE MATTRESS WAS LUMPY. Regis turned her pillow over and rolled over to her side with a sigh. It was no use. It wasn't a lumpy mattress or a flat pillow keeping her awake tonight. Try as she may, she couldn't get her brain to turn off.

Keith was right. She was always running away. Leaving before someone left her. She'd spent years trying to convince herself that she did her job with such dedication because she was passionate about helping people. That's what drove her. Surely Keith could understand that. Why else would he have become a doctor?

As a fresh wave of pain washed over her, she pulled her knees up to her chest and wrapped her arms around them, as if holding them tightly to her would keep her together. For years after David had died, Regis had sworn she'd never allow herself to fall in love like that again. And she hadn't. She never got involved with men when she was on the road, and she was always on the road.

But Keith had worn her down. His gentle smile and easy way had pulled her in right from the start. She didn't understand it. She'd only known Keith for a few weeks. She spent countless nights alone in motel rooms over the years.

And yet, the one thing she knew for sure was that she missed being next to Keith as she slept. She missed the way his hand found her under the blanket and rested on her hip. She missed the way she could feel his warm breath on the back of her neck as he nuzzled against it. And the way his mouth moved perfectly with hers when he kissed her.

Regis turned her face into her pillow and let out a scream of frustration. Every time she closed her eyes, she saw that thick dark hair and remembered how soft it had been between her fingers, saw those amazing eyes and how they'd warmed whenever he'd looked at her.

She'd told him all about David, and he'd known immediately how much she'd loved him. And then realization dawned on Regis like a smack to the head. She shook her head and whispered into the darkness. "That's not possible. I barely know him. We've only been together a few weeks."

Images flashed through her mind in rapid succession.

Deep blue eyes filled with concern as they took in the blood on her leg.

Strong fingers moving gently against her injured flesh.

A warm smile that had greeted her at the door to this very room, just to check on her.

His hand in hers, guiding her as they walked over difficult terrain.

The safety of being wrapped in his arms.

The pain of not having him here with her now.

And then it struck her hard. "What the hell did you do, Reg?" She'd gone and fallen in love with him.

Chapter Ten

REGIS WOKE UP BEFORE her alarm went off; before the sun had even fully breached the horizon. The sky still had that hazy gray, streaked with orange and red that came with morning. She hadn't slept much, but she knew she'd never get back to sleep. Besides, she needed to get to Keith's house before he left for the clinic. What she had to say was important and didn't need to be done in a public place. She grabbed the first clean pair of pants she could get her hands on and yanked on a blouse, buttoning it as she went to her door.

After a quick stop at the diner to grab two coffees, she headed over to Keith's house. But instead of pulling down the driveway, she saw his truck parked in front of the clinic. The light was on inside, but surely it was too early for Nancy to be at work. She parked the car, grabbed the two coffees and walked up the frost-covered ramp to the front door.

The warmth that surged through her the moment she pushed through the door and saw Keith confirmed what she'd been trying to deny. She was in love.

Keith raised his head from whatever he was reading as he sat in the seat normally occupied by Nancy, surprise written on his face at the sight of her. For a split second, Regis felt a twinge of guilt at how ragged he looked, knowing she'd probably caused it. He didn't appear to have gotten any more sleep than she had. Although dressed in a clean shirt and jeans, his hair was tousled more than usual as if he'd spent the last hour pulling his fingers through it with frustration.

Still, the way he looked at her, as if he were drinking her in, made him look incredibly sexy despite his obvious fatigue. Then he smiled. "Are one of those coffees mine?"

A small laugh escaped her lips as she held out the cup, which he reached for through the window that separated Nancy's desk from the waiting room. "Just how you like it. But I didn't make it. Your mother did. I stopped by the diner."

He took a sip of satisfaction. "I needed this."

"I was going to stop by your house. You don't normally come to the clinic this early."

"I couldn't sleep. Seems like that's contagious."

"Can we talk in private?"

He glanced around the room. "No one is here but us, Regis."

She sighed, knowing she was stalling.

"Whatever it is you want to tell me, just say it," he said. "I'm here."

Her bottom lip quivered against all her efforts to stop it. "I know. I'm not used to that."

"Just say it," he urged.

She took a deep, cleansing breath. "I know I've been pushing you away these last few days. I don't know how to do it any other way. I've never had any one place to call home before. I've been running so long, I don't know how to stop."

"This could be your home. Give yourself a reason to love something and dig some roots."

She put her coffee cup down on the table. "It's not that easy."

"It could be." He walked out from behind the desk and came into the waiting room, standing close to her, but not close enough.

Her heart thumped in her chest. "I deal with harsh realities all the time, but the biggest one is how I feel about you. I feel like I'm falling without a safety net. "

"That's what falling in love is. You're not alone." With one quick stride, he was standing in front of her and scooping her into his arms. Here she felt alive and whole. In his arms, she felt the earth beneath her feet.

"We started this, Regis," Keith said, gazing down into her eyes. "Let's finish it. Let's find out how far we can take this. When I went to see you yesterday, I was angry. But I realized last night that it wasn't just about the Buxton Mill claim. We'll figure something out about that. It was because you were leaving, and I didn't know how to feel about that. I've never felt like this before. Since the moment I saw you standing in front of the clinic door, you've been throwing me for a loop. I never knew what love was like. With Logan and Poppy, I saw it. It was real. But I'd never had that before until I met you. I love you, Regis. I'm sure of it."

"I love you, too. I don't know how it happened, but I do."

He kissed her lips, her face and her eyes as he dug his fingers in her hair, setting her soul on fire. It scared her to death and yet, it was everything she wanted.

She heard Nancy clear her throat. *Loudly.*

Keith pulled away from her abruptly and looked up with surprise. When Regis turned, she saw Nancy standing at the door with her coat still on, wearing a grin of amusement. "It's a bit early in the day, isn't it?"

Regis felt her face flame, but Keith wasn't fazed. "Why don't you go to the diner and have a long breakfast. Tell my mother it's on me."

"Oh, Hawk, your mother and I will have plenty to talk about," Nancy said, laughing as she left the office.

Regis giggled. "You do know what they're going to talk about, don't you?"

"I'd hate to disappoint them. I don't expect you to say yes to marriage, Regis. But I can't deny that I hope one day that's what you'll want. All I know is that I don't want you to leave. Please tell me you'll stay."

"I'm almost done with my work here," she said. "I do have that vacation my boss promised—"

"Great," he said, cutting her off. "I'll take however much time I can get with you."

"And then I'll probably be unemployed."

Confusion pulled at his handsome features.

"I think I've figured out a way to help the Buxton Mill center cause."

"Really?"

"I contacted one of the families I lived with on base and mentioned what Ethan and Ian have been trying to do here. It seems there are a lot of groups all over the country who are trying to do the same thing. I've got some great ideas to raise money. It won't be easy, but we may be able to raise the cash needed to make the repairs to the center and even get a grant to complete the renovation. Of course, it puts me out of a job because it'll be a job in itself to facilitate it all. But who knows, we could create a foundation that could grow beyond the Buxton Mills site."

"If it keeps you here in my arms, I'm game if you are."

"We could organize volunteer groups from other counties to come in and do the work in exchange for other services. It would eliminate a lot of red tape. And you know, we could even do that for other people in town to help get the building process started faster."

Keith was staring at her, and she wasn't sure he'd heard a word she'd said.

"Do you think it's too much?" she asked.

He laced his fingers with hers. "I think it's perfect."

She reached up on her toes to kiss him on the mouth. With her lips on his and his fingers entwined with hers, everything felt right.

"I love you Keith McKinnon. But I have only one problem."

A crease pulled at his brow. "What's that?"

"If I don't have a real job anymore, I can't exactly afford to live in the motel."

His smile widened. "Regis Simpson, you will always have a home with me. And I'm going to love you so well you'll never want to leave again."

Regis threw her arms around his neck, hot tears spilling down her cheeks. She buried her face in Keith's neck.

Then he whispered in her ear. "No more leaving. You're home for good."

"I'm going to hold you to that."

Keith's kiss was like a promise full of love and commitment to their future that they would be together always. And for the first time in her life, Regis believed it.

—The End—

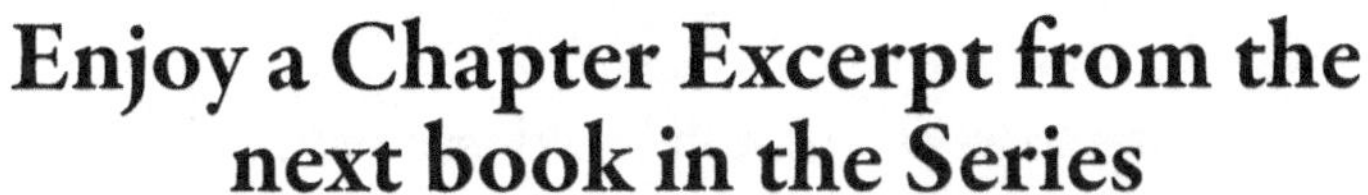

Enjoy a Chapter Excerpt from the next book in the Series

DAKOTA HEAT

HOTSHOT SAM MCKINNON was always leaving town, chasing another fire until his own hometown became vulnerable during the fire season after a big flood left debris and devastation in its path. He didn't expect out of town dispatcher, Summer Bigelow, to catch his eye or his heart.

It hadn't been Summer's idea to move from Providence to South Dakota, but when a serial murderer suddenly turns his attention on Summer, her boss insists she leave town. She's dealt with high tension, life or death situations many times in her job. It isn't until she meets Sam McKinnon and falls for the sexy hotshot that she really begins to know fear. The fear of losing someone she loves.

Chapter One

"YOU'VE GOT TO BE KIDDING." Summer Bigelow glared at the police chief of the Providence Police Department as she sat back against the chair. She'd thought the parking ticket she'd found on her windshield this morning was a bad start to the day, and it could only get better from there.

She'd been wrong.

Matt Jorgensen looked at her with sympathy. "You're one of the best dispatchers I have, Summer. I'm not disputing that."

"Then why?" she said.

Matt raised his voice over hers. "But I'm not going to risk your life to some crazy stalker who has already killed four women."

Summer's mouth dropped open. She forced air into her lungs as she looked at the two detectives sitting in the office with them. Jake Santos and Kevin Gordon had been working this case right from the beginning and had been doing drive-by checks on her ever since the killer had called into her line.

"There was a fourth?"

The grim look they both offered was answer enough.

"Last time he called in, he reported there was a fourth," Jake said. "A kid discovered her taking a shortcut through a parking lot on the way to school this morning."

"But he called in last week. He said ..." Summer fought to think through the chain of events that had transpired over the last two weeks.

Kevin Gordon got up from his seat and walked in front of her, sitting on the desk. She knew his wife had been stalked by her ex-husband a few years ago and was nearly killed.

"You have to take this serious. We are. With Daria, we knew her ex-husband was after her, and she didn't leave town.

We were watching him, and he still managed to slip through our fingers. I thank God every day we found Daria in time. We don't know who this serial killer is or where he'll be next. All we know for sure is that based on his last phone call, he's fixated on you."

"Look at you," Matt said, throwing his pen on the blotter on his desk. "It's been a week since that nutcase called in, and I can already see the toll it's taking on you. You've got dark circles under your eyes, and you look like you haven't slept at all. And don't blame Bobbi's lumpy couch, either. You walk down the hall, and I see you looking over your shoulder. That's no way to live, Summer."

"He doesn't know my name. Bobbi said I could stay at her place as long as I need to while you watch my apartment. How could he possibly find me?"

Jake handed her a folded newspaper. "We found this on your doorstep this morning. He could be anyone you talk to on the street, Summer. Anyone."

She opened the *Providence Journal Bulletin*. In red marker, the words YOU'RE NEXT were boldly scribbled on the page. Taped to the top was a picture of Summer walking out of Bobbi's apartment. The picture had the mark of a bullseye over her face.

Summer swayed in her seat. *The serial killer had been stalking her, and she'd never even known.* The growing ball of fear she'd walked around with for the past week burned in her stomach.

She thought to this morning when she'd found the parking ticket on her car in front of Bobbi's apartment building. A nice man had stopped his walk when she'd ranted in frustration over what was happening and told her the day would get better. It could have been him. *It could be anyone.* How would she know?

"For your own safety," Matt said. "You *are* going to be leaving Providence today. I'm not arguing the point."

"But ... You're sending me to the middle of no man's land."

"South Dakota isn't exactly the South Pole. You'll be working fire dispatch. It's a good cover. I've already briefed the superintendent in charge of the fire unit in the area."

"Fire dispatch."

Matt looked at her file. "You've been trained in it. It's a perfect cover. If the killer continues looking for you, he won't be looking for a fire dispatcher."

"Why would he look for me in South Dakota? What the hell is even in South Dakota?"

Kevin's voice was sobering. "Safety."

"YOU'RE AN ACCIDENT waiting to happen, Sam McKinnon!" Kate McKinnon grabbed the knife out of her son's hand and scowled.

"What am I doing wrong?" Sam asked, chuckling.

Kate grunted with exaggeration. "There are too many things for me to list. Sit down and let me make you a meal, will you? You've been gone for over a year. Can I at least enjoy having you home for five minutes before you blow up my kitchen again?"

"Hey, I told you that was an accident. What did Logan tell you?" Sam said, stepping back against the wall while his mom moved into his spot by the counter.

She waved him off. "Yeah, yeah, never mind. It wasn't always Logan and Ethan creating all the trouble around here. You and your cousin, Ian, were always an unpredictable pair, too." Despite her irritation, Kate chuckled quietly, clearly thrilled to have Sam home after so long.

"I don't have time for one of your famous breakfasts, Ma. I have to meet the new fire crew in an hour."

"You'll be out the door in twenty minutes. Geesh, I wish you'd been this eager to go to school when you were younger."

Kate busied herself whisking scrambled eggs in a cast iron fry pan with one hand while pulling a toasted bagel out of the toaster and dropping it on a clean white plate. She glanced up at Sam with that look she always gave him when she wanted to ask something but wasn't sure if she should.

"What?"

"Speaking of Ian, have you talked to him yet?"

His stomach dropped. His cousin, a wounded military hero, had talked about becoming a Hotshot fireman once he was done with his military service. But a mortar blast in Afghanistan had left him without a leg and struggling to find his way again back home.

"I just got home last night. Haven't had a chance."

Kate smiled weakly. "He'll be happy to see you. Just don't avoid him because you think it's too painful for him. He'd hate that."

Sam leaned back in his chair. His brother Ethan had told him as much. Ethan, a former Navy Seal, understood what Ian was going through more than any of them.

"I'll make sure I stop by on my way home today."

Smiling, Kate placed a full plate of food in front of Sam along with a full glass of orange juice.

"If you keep feeding me like this, Ma, I'll be so fat I won't be able to get any of my fire gear on by the end of the week."

There was a twinkle of happiness in her eyes as his mother smiled down at him. "If that's what it takes to keep my boy home in Rudolph, I'm game. If I can manage to find you a girl, even better."

THE GIRL WAS NEW. Sam walked around the Interagency Fire Crew basecamp with familiarity. He saw faces he recognized from working in different locations over the past few years. But the girl ... Yeah, she was new. He doubted he would forget the soft blonde color of her hair or the slight tilt of her head as she read through paperwork, pretending she didn't notice the people around her.

He grabbed two water bottles from the bucket full of ice in the back of the Quonset hut and walked toward her. She didn't look up until he held the water bottle in front of her.

Blue eyes met his with a mixture of irritation and surprise.

"You're dropping ice pieces on my paperwork," she said.

He noticed the smooth as silk sound of her voice before the water splatter on the top page of her paperwork. He immediately pulled the water bottle back a few inches.

"Sorry. I thought you might like something to drink."

Her face softened as quickly as it had shown irritation. She reached her hand out and took the water bottle, and then placed it on the bench next to her before shaking her hand of the residual moisture the bottle left behind. "Thank you."

"You're new here," he said as he sat down next to her.

Not looking up, she said, "So are you."

She smelled like soap and lavender. After breathing in smoke and dirt for so long, it was refreshing to breathe in the sweet scents of a woman.

"Not exactly. I grew up in Rudolph."

That earned him a lingering second glance. One that afforded him a few seconds to really look into her eyes, at her face.

"Really?"

"My whole life."

She glanced around quickly. "When I got in last night I was told the basecamp here was new this year. I didn't realize South Dakota had a dedicated fire basecamp."

Sam had never worked fire duty in his home state before. And he'd never come to a new location and been so familiar with faces as well as the location. His reason for wanting to come back to South Dakota this year was personal.

A lot of his friends who worked with the Interagency Fire Crew were still reeling after the deaths of nineteen Hotshot firemen in Arizona last summer. Some had quit fighting fires altogether at the urging of their family. Sam's own mother had tried her best to do the same during many phone calls since the tragedy, but Kate McKinnon settled for having him come home to Rudolph to work.

"This was just constructed this year. The Black Hills are a hot spot this year because of all the flood and ice damage that occurred over the winter. When I found out they were setting up a base here to do fire control for the season, I put in a request to work here."

She nodded. "Must be nice to be home. At least for the season."

She glanced down at her paperwork again.

He chuckled at how quickly she fell into her reading again. "You're looking at that like you're cramming for a final exam."

She shrugged. "I feel I am. This is my first season working fire dispatch anywhere."

"Ah, then that explains it."

"Must feel good to be home after—"

"Summer?"

Both Sam and the girl looked up to see the chief calling out from across the tent. The girl quickly collected her paperwork and stuffed it in a folder.

"Be right there," she called out. She turned to Sam, lifting the bottled water in her hand. "Thanks for the water."

"No problem."

But she was already trotting over to the superintendent's office. He hadn't even had a chance to get her name. But he would before the day was done. This was one woman he had a feeling he wanted to get to know.

ADAM WHITE SAT DOWN at his desk and glanced at the folder Summer had handed him. She'd been given strict orders to report immediately to the superintendent of the Interagency Fire Crew she'd been assigned to on her first day on the job.

Summer hated first days on the job. The butterflies that had been souring her stomach for the past two days as she drove from Providence to Rudolph were only getting worst. She'd barely had enough time to get herself settled in the basecamp housing let alone look at the portfolio of information she'd been given when she'd been booted out of the police station.

She'd left her meeting with the chief to find Bobbi had already packed her bags and loaded them in her car. Matt had handed her an itinerary and given her an envelope full of petty cash, courtesy of an officer collection at the precinct. It didn't take a genius to know Bobbi had been behind it. Her friend had been worried sick about her ever since the call came in on her phone line from the serial killer, telling her he was watching her.

When she'd counted the money, she'd gasped, not knowing whether to be flattered that the officers in the department cared that much about her well-being, or be offended that they wanted her out of town so badly. Since Bobbi had been on duty when she left, Summer hadn't had time to thank her friend for all she'd done for her before Summer left the city.

Adam finally closed the folder and handed it to her. "Did you find everything you need last night?"

"Uh, yeah. I guess."

"Good. It's the dormitory is rudimentary but has everything you'll need for the time being. I was told that some of the local rooms at the motel in town might open up soon now that some of the emergency crew that came into town over the winter will be leaving. You might find it more comfortable there."

"No, it's fine."

"We have briefings every day in the room you were in earlier. Most of the fire crew is required to do an hour of physical training every day, but that's not necessary for your job in dispatch. But feel free to use to the equipment in the

Quonset hut if you want. I just ask that you wait until most of the crew has done their daily workout."

"Sure."

Adam stood up from his seat behind the desk and glanced quickly out the window at the crew of fire fighters who had already arrived. The briefing room she'd sat in earlier would soon be full of Hotshot fire fighters.

"Matt and I go way back to college. I was glad to get his call about you doing dispatch for us this fire season. Even though this is your first season in fire dispatch, Matt has high regard for your instinct and dedication. I think you'll do fine here."

"Thank you."

Despite being close to the same age as the police chief in Providence, Adam looked older, with salt and pepper hair and deep creases around his eyes. She guessed him to be close to forty, or maybe a few years beyond. As he looked at her, his forehead creased.

"What are you holding back?" she said.

He chuckled. "Matt warned me about you. Very direct. That's good. I just wanted to say that no one knows about what's going on back in Providence but me. Matt would like it to stay that way. I'll be checking in with him each week just for peace of mind. He'll keep me abreast of what is going on there if anything happens in the meantime. All I want you to do is concentrate on settling in. I see you've already met our squad leader, Sam McKinnon."

"Excuse me?"

"The man you were talking to in the briefing room when I first arrived."

How could she forget? Summer forced herself to be as nonchalant as she could. "Oh, him."

Adam chuckled.

"What?"

"I'm not sure he's used to that kind of brush off from women. He's got the reputation of being a bit of a charmer with the ladies. Don't say you didn't notice."

Her mouth dropped open. "He only handed me a bottle of water. We didn't even have a chance to exchange names before you called me in here."

Adam smiled knowingly.

"I'm sure that will change. Sam likes to know the people he's working with. It doesn't surprise me at all he sought you out before I had a chance to introduce you to the crew. He is one of the best Hotshots I've worked with. He doesn't let anything get in the way of doing his job safely."

She nodded. "Then I guess we'll get along fine."

Purchase DAKOTA HEAT[1]

---

1. https://books2read.com/u/me078E

Ebooks by Lisa Mondello

DAKOTA HEARTS SERIES
Her Dakota Man,[1] book 1
Badland Bride,[2] book 2
Dakota Heat,[3] book 3
Wild Dakota Heart,[4] book 4
His Dakota Bride,[5] book 5
Dakota Wedding,[6] book 6
His Dakota Heart,[7] book 7
Dakota Cowboy,[8] book 8
One Dakota Night,[9] book 9
Dakota Homecoming,[10] book 10
Dakota Christmas, book 11[11]

---

1. https://books2read.com/u/mqzg88

2. https://books2read.com/u/31gY1W

3. https://books2read.com/u/me078E

4. https://books2read.com/u/mVEP53

5. https://books2read.com/u/3JKRNJ

6. https://books2read.com/u/47jYEm

7. https://books2read.com/u/bQZdE0

8. https://books2read.com/u/mBn5Mm

9. https://books2read.com/u/bWKPy7

10. https://books2read.com/u/bMGXlG

11. http://littl.ink/+dwAm

Dakota Hearts Complete Set 1-10[12]
HEROES OF PROVIDENCE SERIES
Material Witness, Book 1[13]
(**Named one of Kirkus Reviews Best Books of 2012)
Safe Haven, Book 2[14]
Reckless Hours, Book 3[15]
Desperate Hours, Book 4[16]
Final Hours, Book 5[17]
Cold Harbor, Book 6[18]
TEXAS HEARTS SERIES
Texas Hearts Box Set 1-3[19]
Her Heart for the Asking, Book 1[20]
His Heart for the Trusting, Book 2[21]
The More I See, Book 3[22]
Gypsy Hearts, Book 4
Leaving Liberty, Book 5[23]
His Texas Heart, Book 6[24]

---

12. https://books2read.com/u/bza1Kj

13. https://books2read.com/u/4N1X5J

14. https://books2read.com/u/4DAgrk

15. https://books2read.com/u/3GMA7O

16. https://books2read.com/u/3yPz2p

17. https://books2read.com/u/38DVna

18. https://books2read.com/u/4EWNpO

19. https://books2read.com/u/mqz0aZ

20. https://books2read.com/u/m0zwdM

21. https://books2read.com/u/3RBnlx

22. https://books2read.com/u/mvYnz2

23. https://books2read.com/u/mlK2GW

24. https://books2read.com/u/bxgjPe

The Wedding Dress, Book 7[25]
Lone Star Lady, Book 8[26]
Under a Texas Star, book 9[27]
Lone Star Hero, book 10

FATE WITH A HELPING HAND SERIES

Tempting Fate Box Set 1-3[28]
The Gift, Prequel[29]
All I Want for Christmas is You, Book 1[30]
The Marriage Contract, Book 2[31]
The Knight and Maggie's Baby, Book 3[32]
My Lucky Charm, Book 4[33]

SUMMER HOUSE SERIES

Moment in Time, Book 1[34]
Moment of Impact, Book 2[35]
Moment of Truth, Book 3[36]
Moment of Trust, Book 4[37]

CONTEMPORARY WESTERN ROMANCE

---

25. https://books2read.com/u/bxgjPe

26. https://books2read.com/u/mlK89Y

27. https://books2read.com/u/47kLY7

28. https://books2read.com/u/mdKnAd

29. https://books2read.com/u/3ne8y5

30. https://books2read.com/u/47klLg

31. https://books2read.com/u/4jKLp5

32. https://books2read.com/u/bzpgAn

33. https://books2read.com/u/3RBnDx

34. http://summerhouseseries.blogspot.com/p/moment-in-time.html

35. http://summerhouseseries.blogspot.com/p/moment-of-impact.html

36. http://summerhouseseries.blogspot.com/p/blog-page.html

37. http://summerhouseseries.blogspot.com/p/blog-page_7.html

<u>Nothing But Trouble</u>[38]
RODEO KNIGHTS SERIES
<u>Her Knight, Her Protector</u>, Book 1 by Lisa Mondello[39]
SWEET MONTANA SERIES
<u>Sweet Montana Sky</u> (also part of the Rodeo Knights collection)[40]
Never miss a new release by Lisa Mondello. Sign up for my new release newsletter at http://eepurl.com/xhxO5
For up to date information on new releases, visit me at www.lisamondello.com[41] or write me at LisaMondello@aol.com.

---

38. https://books2read.com/u/mgKz8R

39. https://books2read.com/u/bP1Xlz

40. https://books2read.com/u/mqzYBO

41. http://www.lisamondello.com

Don't miss out!

Visit the website below and you can sign up to receive emails whenever Lisa Mondello publishes a new book. There's no charge and no obligation.

https://books2read.com/r/B-A-CEU-FPIH

BOOKS 2 READ

Connecting independent readers to independent writers.